FIC   Clarke, Terence.

             The king of Rumah
             Nadai.

$18.95

DATE			

AUG   1994

BAKER & TAYLOR

The King of Rumah Nadai

MERCURY HOUSE

The
King
of
Rumah
Nadai

Terence
Clarke

SAN FRANCISCO

Published in the United States by
Mercury House
San Francisco, California

Cover art by Mark Johnson. Interior illustrations digitally adapted from cover art by Thomas Christensen.

United States Constitution, First Amendment: Congress shall make no law respecting an establishment of religion, or prohibiting the free exercise thereof; or abridging the freedom of speech, or of the press; or the right of the people peaceably to assemble, and to petition the Government for a redress of grievances.

Mercury House and colophon are registered trademarks of
Mercury House, Incorporated

Printed on acid-free paper
Manufactured in the United States of America

Library of Congress Cataloging-in-Publication Data

Clarke, Terence.
    The king of Rumah Nadai / Terence Clarke.
      p.   cm.
    ISBN 1-56279-060-9 (cloth) :
      1. Culture conflict—Borneo—Fiction. 2. Ibans
(Bornean people)—Fiction. 3. Americans—Borneo
—Fiction. I. Title.
PS3553.L338K56 1994
813'.54—dc20   93-40233
                                    CIP

5   4   3   2   1

For Alev Lytle Croutier

He was there in the wilderness …
and was with the wild beasts.

—Mark

1

The facade of His Majesty's Arms was white, though mottled with age and the slime residue of innumerable monsoons. The doors and all the trim of the hotel were painted dirty green, like smudges of avocado. The coconut palms in the yard hung exhausted in the afternoon heat. From a distance, Collins thought, the blank face of the building looking out on the Kuching River resembled that of a seedy, unwashed Englishman.

The building had sunk a few inches into the riverbank mud. The entryway sagged to the right, and the two wooden doors did not appear capable of swinging at all. To Collins's surprise, though, the doors did open, leading to a large porch that was bound across the front and sides by a long rusted screen. The doors had been trimmed at the bottom to accommodate the hotel's lean. Collins noticed that the carpentry work had also provided an avenue for the entry of a cloud of mosquitos.

The plank floor inclined

unevenly, in many directions. Collins imagined that, if you dropped a marble onto the floor, it would roll, in random meanders, forever. The main stairway at the rear of the lobby leaned to the left, and indeed the left side of the stairs made up a kind of rutted path like those Collins had seen in the jungle. To the left, beyond the reservation desk, a dining hall looked out onto the river. On the right, an equally large sitting room was furnished with an overstuffed couch, a metal card table, and four metal chairs. The couch was brown, though its arms had faded to a dustlike color, about the same as cement. A photo of Her Royal Highness Queen Elizabeth II was pinned to the wall above an empty watercooler. She was reading a speech, and her crown seemed to be held up by the intent furrows on her brow. There was also a newspaper photo of Elizabeth Taylor done up as Cleopatra.

Collins lowered his suitcase to the floor.

—May I help you, Mister?

The voice was grainy with age. A very dark Tamil man stood in the doorway to the dining hall, holding a white towel. His white jacket appeared crisp and correct, but Collins noticed it was missing a button and that there was a stain on one sleeve. At first, the American guessed the stain was soup. Curry, perhaps. But as the waiter approached, Collins saw it was a splotch of rust from one of the screens.

—Did the boy from the Hotel Kuching come here, Collins asked, —to let you know I was coming?

—I don't know, Mister, the man said. —And, I'm afraid the clerk is at tea. I can be of use, perhaps?

—Thank you, yes, I …

—My name is John, the man interrupted as he motioned Collins toward the reservations desk. —My father lived and died here in Kuching, he added, walking behind the counter and sitting down at a painted, wooden desk. —So, he should have called me Kamanan or Itaikkunrurkilar or one of those, I suppose.

—Uh, I guess so.

John opened the center drawer. —Ah! here it is! He pulled a ledger book from the drawer and brought it to the counter. —But my father admired the English, he continued, opening the book. —... Like so many of us here in Sarawak. So I was christened John Bull Porvaikkiperunarkilli.

He extended a hand. —And you are?

—Dan.

John's damp fingers held onto the American's hand as he looked into the book.

—Dan Collins.

—Ah yes, here you are, he said. —Three nights?

Collins nodded, and John turned the ledger about and asked him to sign his name. —Your passport, please.

He folded his towel and laid it next to the book.

—The law, you know, he said, as Collins completed the paperwork. —It puts the government off if we let you stay here without proper identification.

—Yes, I know. Collins heard the testiness in his own voice, but allowed it to remain. John had nothing to do with Collins's current problems, but his insistent politeness somehow furthered the American's fear that he was here in Kuching because he had done wrong, and that the meeting that was to be held the next day was all his fault.

—Ah. You've visited Borneo before, John said, sensing Collins's impatience.

—I've lived here for five years, John.

The smile fell from the Indian's face. —Oh. Sorry. He took up the towel once more.

Collins removed the passport from his shoulder bag and opened it. It was new, obtained a few months earlier from the embassy in Kuala Lumpur.

He disliked the photo of himself. In the years since he had received his first State Department passport, in 1963, he had grown bedraggled. The skin around his eyes resembled a much-folded map. His curly black hair remained, but now it was longer and, to his surprise, rather unkempt. Collins had never been a neat man. His personal appearance was a matter of running a comb—occasionally—through his hair. But especially now that he ran the Agency for International Development station in Sarawak and was, therefore, a senior representative of the U.S. Department of State, he did think that he had a duty to keep up an official appearance. An American diplomat. Shaggy hair was not diplomatic. Nor was the sense Collins had just now of his own vulnerability. His worry about the meeting the next day made him feel as though he were going nuts, and he figured he must look nuts as well.

—Excuse me, John. I didn't mean to be rude, he said. —It's just that ...

—You've come a long way.

John's teeth were extraordinarily white. Collins realized they were false and, moreover, new.

—Perhaps you would allow me to make you some tea?

Collins nodded and wrote down his passport number in the ledger. —That's very kind of you, he said.

—And toast, as well?

—Yes, thanks.

—With some proper Robertson's Marmalade?

—Terrific.

Collins took up his bag and carried it to the dining hall. There were a dozen tables, all set with white tablecloths and heavy, much-polished silverware. Each table had a salt and pepper set of white ceramic that commemorated the visit to Kuching of His Majesty the Prince of Wales in 1931. A drawing of the prince in dress military uniform decorated the salt shaker. A similar drawing, of another white man, was on the pepper shaker. To the left of the entry, a large green parrot sat on his perch surrounded by broken sunflower seeds. Collins sat down at a table with a clear view of the river, although all the tables had such a view, the dining room being empty.

A moment later, John entered the dining hall with a pot of tea, a plate of toast, and a jar of jam. He bustled about Collins, making sure he was taken care of.

—John, how old is this hotel?

—It was dedicated in 1921. By Rajah Charles Vyner Brooke himself. John took up the pepper shaker and indicated the drawing. —This chap here.

—And how long have you been here?

John bowed tightly. —Since that very day. I was a boy, a student in the Missionary English school. Forty-seven years ago.

—And what was your first job here at the hotel?

Again John bowed. —Just this, he said, spreading his arms out to take in the entire dining hall.

—It's been busy?

—Yes. There was a pause. —It was.

—But there doesn't seem to be anyone here just now.

—This week, there is no one. John took the cloth napkin from the table, opened it, and spread it across Collins's lap. —Next week perhaps there will be someone.

He folded his hands before him. His head inclined to the side, and his dark eyes searched the tabletop mournfully.

—It is because nothing good happens here any more, he said.

—At His Majesty's Arms?

—No, Mister. In Borneo. John shook his head. —When the White Rajahs were here, it was a festive time. Celebrations year round. Happiness, you know. There was none of this racialism and suspicion.

John looked over his shoulder, as though concerned that someone may be overhearing his lament.

—No communists, for one. The Chinese embraced the Muslim, the Muslim took the Tamil's hand. All, all was peaceful.

Collins, a piece of toast in his hand, had no reply. The passion of John's description made Borneo sound like heaven.

—And none of those, John sniffed, indicating two men at a corner table of the dining room. Both were sweating heavily and sat tipsily before an open bottle of Hennessy cognac, humming an odd, summer-camp–sounding tune. They wore white kimonos.

—Hmph. Japanese, John continued. —Although these two are the first we've had here since 1945, when, well …

John gestured, looking for commiseration from Collins.

—Different circumstances, naturally, Collins said.

John motioned toward the two men across the room. —And these are businessmen, I understand. Imagine! Japanese businessmen. Not English businessmen. The White Rajahs must be rolling in their graves, poor blokes.

Though Collins savored the hot tea John had brought him, he wished he had been able to get a room at the Hotel Kuching, where he normally stayed. But every room there was booked, and the manager, an Englishman named Arthur Edison, had suggested His Majesty's Arms as an alternative.

—Not up to our standards, of course, Edison had told him. —But the staff is presentable, and the sheets washed.

—You're sure you don't have a spare room? Collins had asked.

—I'm afraid not, Edison said, looking once more at the room keys hanging from the hooks behind the desk. —The trouble is, there are several of your countrymen staying here.

—They're here? Collins inquired, looking over his shoulder.

—Yes. Serious lot, aren't they, your government? They come here speaking that odd lingo, in those short-sleeved dress shirts, with neckties, God help us—neckties, in Borneo!—and every one of them looking like that chap who was your President a few years ago. You know, the Irishman. Kennedy, poor man.

—Yes, yes.

—Must you Americans wear your hair that way? Edison flashed the brief smile that Collins knew served as the Englishman's laughter.

—Of course not, Collins replied. —I don't wear my hair that way.

—I know, Dan. And the Irish in London don't either. But something happens to them when they go to the States.

—I wouldn't know, Collins muttered. He looked into the bar, fearful he would be spotted by Joseph Feeney, the State Department officer he had been told was coming to talk to him. Edison noticed his anxiety.

—Oh, no, they're not here now, he said. —They went out for lunch, I think. Excited about it, too, they were. None of them appeared to have ever been here before.

—Good. And now that they've seen it, I hope they'll leave.

—You don't want to visit with your friends?

Collins took up his bag. —Thanks, Arthur. Just don't tell them I was here.

—Well, fine, old boy, if you say so.

Collins turned and left the hotel.

The room he had at His Majesty's Arms, like all of them on the second floor, looked out on a hallway that circuited the hotel. The hallway was screened, and his view of the river, glistening pink in the late afternoon, contained all the garish colors that made the sunsets in Sarawak so unbelievable. Collins thought that, were he to paint the sunsets, with the blues and violently changing reds and yellows that they contained every day, he would be laughed at for being a caricaturist. Just now, a reeling canopy of narrow clouds, like curved contrails one next to another, hung over the river. They were gold at the horizon and, high over the water, blood-red, with the sky beyond a sort of blood-blue. There was no subtlety in any of it. The sun seemed to have heaved toward the earth and exploded.

John came up the hall with a tray, on which was balanced a second pot of tea and a jug of water. Two towels hung over his sleeve. He wore black loafers and no socks. The cuffs of his white pants were ragged but clean.

—Here you are, Mister.

—Thanks, John. Listen, I may be getting some messages from a man named Mr. Feeney.

—Yes?

—And it's important that I be able to call him when it suits me. That is, see, I don't want to be surprised by him.

—Sorry?

—I mean … it's this. Collins thrust his empty hand into a pocket. —If I'm here at the hotel, and this fellow Feeney … or any American, for that matter … comes here wanting to see me, I want you to tell them I'm not here.

John stared a moment at the teapot. Collins reached into his shoulder bag and took out a ten *ringgit* bill, which he folded and held in his hand.

—You want me to tell a lie? John asked.

—Yes. I suppose you could say that.

—This chap is a government officer?

—Yes.

—I would not be punished.

—Of course not. Collins held out his hand, exposing the edges of the folded bill.

—Is this man an enemy, Mister? John asked. His eyes fell to the money.

—No.

Immediately John took the bill and shoved it into his coat pocket.

Startled by the sudden movement, Collins replied, —Actually, he's my boss.

—You work for him? John shook his head, then held the towels out before him, handing them to Collins. —You can do this to a boss in America? Fool him?

—No, John, it's not that. It's just that …

—In our civil service one would be sacked for such a thing.

The look of worry that appeared in John's face caused his skin

to darken. All of a sudden, the grizzle of his beard looked quite ancient. He glanced toward Collins's shoulder bag, his eyebrows rising inquisitively. Collins took out another bill and passed it to John, who, once more, snatched it from him.

—But if you insist, Tuan, John muttered.

—Thank you.

An hour later, Collins descended once again into the dining room, his fresh shirt and shorts wrinkled from his suitcase. The bath he had taken had relaxed him, and, sitting at the same table with a bottle of cold Tiger Beer, he looked out at the water and tried to assess what had happened during the previous few days.

Though the AID office was in the American consulate in Kuching, Collins had been living for the past few months a hundred miles north, in Simanggang. A team of Americans was advising the Malaysians on the gravel highway link being built to the southern bank of the Rajang River. It was the biggest project the Agency had ever done in Sarawak, and Collins had wanted to keep an eye on it personally.

Returning one afternoon to the house he had rented, he had gotten a message to contact the AID office in Kuala Lumpur as soon as possible.

Radio-telephone, if necessary, the note had read.

Collins had driven down from the project in his Land Rover and was covered with sweat. His legs were colored orange by the caked mud in which he had been working all day. After a quick bath he walked to the District Office where, after a half-hour wait, the Malay who operated the radio-telephone finally got through.

—Very difficult, Tuan, the man said, handing him the phone.

—Radio waves maybe don't go so well over the real waves.

Kuala Lumpur, the capital of Malaysia, was three hundred miles to the west, across the South China Sea.

Despite the rough transmission, the voice on the other end was remarkably clear. It was that of Tully Spencer, the man in charge of the Agency for all of Malaysia.

—Dan, what the hell is it with this guy up the Baleh River?

Collins let a breath wander from his lungs.

—What the hell's Eddie Gould doing up there?

Collins leaned forward. All the Malay office workers watched him, unused to so large an American sprawled so unevenly over the counter.

—He's working for the Agency, Tully, Collins said. —What do you think?

—You know, Dan, Spencer said. —What I just asked you wasn't the question the fellows in Washington asked me.

—Oh, Collins muttered. —Washington saw him in *National Geographic*.

—Yes, they saw him, dammit. How could they miss him, dressed in a loincloth, tattooed all over—and on the cover, no less?

—On the cover.

—Right. And the question was, Who's the dumb shit that let that guy stay up there? Dan, that was the question.

Collins groaned.

—So I told them the truth.

—Of course, Collins replied. —You said …

—I told them it was you.

Collins reached into his shirt pocket for a packet of Lucky Strikes. Taking one out, he tapped it on the counter and placed it between his lips. Quickly, one of the Malays stood, pulled a lighter from his pants pocket, and lit Collins's cigarette. He waved his hand before him in a gesture of thanks.

—Who was it that asked?

—Joseph Feeney.

—Feeney!

—That's right, Dan. The Undersecretary of State for Southeast Asian Affairs. He's visiting Kuala Lumpur just now.

There was a long crackle on the radio-telephone, and for a moment Collins could not hear Spencer's voice. The line cleared.

—And he told me to get you into Kuching next week, because he's coming to visit you, Spencer concluded.

—Do they want Eddie there, too?

—Yes. That's why I'm flying over to Sarawak tomorrow.

—You?

—I've got to go up and get him.

—To take him out of the jungle?

—That's it. We can't have one of our people on the cover of *National Geographic* looking like a damned native. Like a damned Iban headhunter, Dan. You should have known that.

—But you have to at least talk to Eddie before you …

—That's what I'm going to do! I'm going to give him a minute to explain himself, and then I'm going to get him out of there.

—Collins brought the cigarette to his lips once more. —OK. I'll go with you.

—You can't.

—Why?

Again there was a sputter of static, and Collins strained to hear.

—They told me … they told me to do it myself, Spencer said, —and to keep you out of it, because they aren't sure how stable you are.

—Me!

—That's right. I mean, they think it's pretty foolish of you to have let that situation get out of hand over there.

—But …

—So now I've got to go up and get him.

For a moment, neither man spoke. Finally Spencer's voice came over once more.

—What's it like up that river? he asked.

Collins leaned his forehead on the palm of one hand. The smoke from the cigarette swirled in his hair as he recalled his own trip to Rumah Bintang, the chill of the mist from the falls above the longhouse, the rough-hewn house a graceless, lovely anomaly in the forest.

—It's different from anything you've ever seen, he said.

—Dangerous?

—Yes. As Collins replied, a few seconds of static cluttered the line.

—What? What was that?

—Yes, it's dangerous, Tully. Very dangerous.

2

Six months earlier, Collins had been at a rear table in the Five Emerald Goddess, a noodle cafe on Merdeka Street in Kuching, beaming with satisfaction.

—I guess we're just damned glad to have him, he said.

—A fellow like Eddie . . . , Joe Salt agreed. —As good as he is . . . in a situation like that, you couldn't have a better man.

Salt fingered the glass of Tiger Beer on the table before him. At the rear of the cafe, the chef, an acquaintance of Collins's named Ah Woo, stirred a mixture of shredded chicken and green beans, tossing it quickly from his wok into a white crockery dish. He had greeted the two Americans in English when they entered the cafe. —Good-bye, he had said. It was his only English. Now, he moved so rapidly from order to order that he appeared automated. He shouted at the two waiters. The rattle in his voice underscored the fervor of his cooking.

—Eddie's the best I've ever seen out here, Salt grinned. The photographer was of medium height, thin, with defined musculature and extremely curly hair. He was dressed in a green T-shirt, khaki shorts, and sandals. A scuffed thirty-five millimeter Leica camera lay on the table next to the teapot. He had been visiting on assignment from the *National Geographic,* and he claimed his article about the new nation of Malaysia, with the state of Sarawak as its centerpiece, had almost written itself. He had gotten Collins's name from Agency headquarters in Washington, and it had been Collins who had suggested he go up the Baleh River to visit Eddie Gould. It turned out to have been wise advice. Eddie had provided the impulse for the last section of the piece Salt had written and photographed. It was about the Peace Corps, the Agency for International Development, and other examples of American largesse—and how they were bringing light to the jungles of Borneo.

—You ought to go see him yourself, Salt said. —It'd be a treat.

Collins was inclined to do so. In Sarawak, where the Peace Corps had a large presence, his own more professional and capable AID people had received short shrift. Since they were regular State Department officials, they seldom sought publicity as the Peace Corps did. And he knew that this article would not be a problem. The *National Geographic* was so respectable a magazine that he could not imagine anything untoward appearing in it. He sipped his beer as the waiter placed the chicken dish before him.

—I think I will, Collins said. —It's a pleasure to hear about people like Eddie. Doesn't always happen.

Salt laid his chopsticks on the table. His eyebrows rose.

—Sometimes, you know, you put people out there by themselves, Collins explained —and it results in a kind of ... well, disintegration. Nothing serious, of course. Sometimes it's a retreat. They read books all day instead of doing what they're supposed to do. Or they don't do anything instead of doing what they're supposed to do.

Collins looked out to the sidewalk. A crowd of Malay students passed up the street. They were dressed in white shirts, dark blue shorts, and sandals—their school uniform. There was a languid pleasure about their passing. Their dark skin and black hair gave soft contrast to the noise of traffic and bustle from the potholed street.

—Most of our people, of course, do better than that, Collins continued. He spooned a pile of chicken from the dish and laid it next to the white rice on the plate. —You've finished your article?

—That's right, Salt replied. He pulled his canvas bag from the floor and set it on the table beside his plate of rice. —And I've got the film right here.

He smiled broadly. His curly hair appeared electrified against the water-stained wall behind him.

—I'm going to try to get him on the cover, Salt enthused —and if I do that, Eddie'll be famous. He placed the Leica in the shoulder bag. —It'll be terrific, he said. He reached across to the platter and spooned some chicken onto his plate, gravy inundating the rice like a dark blanket. —Eddie Gould! He waved the spoon in the air. —Adventurer!

Collins smiled at the idea as well, actually wishing he were in Eddie's place, celebrated for his valorous work in the jungle. It sounded so romantic, and Collins was pleased by the notion that he had had so much to do with Eddie's unique situation. After all, Eddie Gould was essentially just a bureaucrat. A civil engineer, like Collins himself.

He recalled the AID job announcements he had read years ago, plain pieces of white paper filled with information about government pay levels, vacation leave, length of service. There had been little difference between the announcements Collins had read for Borneo and those for any other place. But above all there had been nothing in them about what was to be found out here *beyond* the reach of the Department of State. Nothing, Collins had later found, about oppressive heat, or the sudden appearance, deep in the forest, of children sheltering themselves from the rain beneath giant ferns. Of monsoon rivers rising forty feet during the night. Of the way the water in the rivers offers little relief from the jungle air, both of similar make-up and almost the same temperature. The announcements were filled with plainspoken data, while Borneo itself, and its heat, brought you odd sicknesses and revelations.

Even as a child Collins had loved reading about explorers and great adventurers. A photo of a British hunter in a pith helmet would fill him with a kind of longing ... to be standing there with the man, surveying the hulk of a collapsed water buffalo, proud to have brought it down with a single shot. The locale of such adventures had not mattered to Collins. New Guinea's wild black men, bones sticking from their noses, made his mind wander as happily as did Edmund Hillary's ascent of Everest.

For some years after his graduation from the University of California, Collins's office at AB Engineering Systems in San Francisco housed just his drawing table—one of several in the same large white room—his drawing tools, a slide rule, and his stool. The single decoration had been a wall calendar from Molinari's Delicatessen on Columbus Avenue. The light coming through the windows had carried the sound of traffic from the street, and there was the dry roar of urban noise all the time.

Collins became a project supervisor after a while, which took him out of the office and provided work he really enjoyed. The big pieces of equipment on the projects seemed like huge yellow monsters to him, scratching at the earth and shoving it around. That order could come from the mess of a large site always amused him. At first, there was a vast lot filled with mud, a swath of total destruction and chaos. Then, slowly, like a phoenix rising into the blue elevations, a new overpass! Despite all this, Collins sighed at how the changes that occurred in his life seemed so predictable. He ate and worked. He made money like everybody else. He bought a set of flats in North Beach, and he was once engaged to be married. At the age of thirty-two, he was named a partner in the firm. He was humorous. His talents were sought after.

Then, one day, he wrote to Washington on a whim. Let's just see what they've got, he thought to himself. A lovely vision had entered Collins's mind, that of an agonized sunset wrapping itself about a dark grove of palm trees along a beach on … let's see, he thought, which one? … on the South China Sea.

When, after several months' correspondence, an offer came through from the Agency for International Development, Collins took it immediately.

So it was that he started reading about Borneo. He was fascinated by it all. James Brooke, for example, the nineteenth-century English adventurer who had subdued native uprisings for the Sultan of Borneo in his southern territories. The first uprising lasted until the moment Brooke fired the field-piece that rested on the foredeck of his sailing ship, and the warring Ibans ran off into the woods. With his victory, Sir James demanded the territory he had just liberated. Subsequent skirmishes, all of which were subdued by Brooke, resulted in subsequent demands for more land. The five parcels granted to him, called divisions, came to make up the country of Sarawak, which remained the private possession of the Brooke family for about a hundred years. After the Japanese war, the British government took it over, and now Sarawak formed one of the easternmost states of the new nation of Malaysia.

Collins read all sorts of things about Sarawak and its forests, which were like vast vegetative warrens housing so many different people. He saw photos of the Malays and Chinese who lived in this part of Borneo. More important, he saw pictures of the tribes. Those people, the people Brooke had defeated, living in the outback in longhouses that contained sometimes a thousand inhabitants, stared back at him from the books he read, covered with tattoos, their teeth black with the ravages of betel nut. Closely woven, tiny straw quivers clung to their loincloths, quivers that contained blowgun darts, charms, parts of luck-providing animals. Looking at the pictures, Collins could actually feel the blood running through his heart, driven by some kind of watery light, cleansing him.

He pictured himself standing among a group of these people, quite a bit bigger than any of them. In fact, in his imagination, he looked like a giant, his shirt ragged and blousy with sweat. The ground around him was strewn with broken ferns and branches, and he noted that his boots sunk into the mud. Then he saw himself dressed as the Ibans were. His white skin gleamed beneath his tattoos. One of the books he read had actually showed the tattoos being applied by an Iban artist, and Collins winced as he imagined the dye-soaked needle tapping his shoulder, leaving a parquetlike, scabbed design in blue and dark red. His earlobes were stretched to his shoulders, the brass rings resting against his collarbones. And his hair was quite long down the back as he stood like a bumpkin staring into the camera. He appeared somewhat mad.

Not at all, he thought, like the suave Sir Richard Burton in Mecca. But he also appeared happy. Besides, a gorgeous hornbill bird was perched on Collins's shoulder. Its black and white feathers were like somber robes beneath the maroon-red dark beak.

The day Collins arrived in Sarawak, in 1963, he was greeted at the Kuching airport by a Malay holding a sign that misspelled his name. A squall was, at that moment, making its way across the tarmac, and the American was awash with sweat and rain as they made their way toward the baggage area. He covered his head with the copy of the *New York Times* he had brought with him. By the time they reached the airport building, the paper had turned to a thick, paginated goo, speckled black. He threw it away.

The Malay introduced himself as Saladin bin Abdul. He weighed about ninety pounds. His face was very dark and covered with age lines. There were pouches at either end of his mouth. His lightly tinted sunglasses reminded Collins of photos he had seen of Malaysian government ministers, although it was evident from his threadbare, but quite clean, shirt that Saladin was not a highly placed official. He wore flip-flops. He shook Collins's hand, then placed his hand against his chest, nodding slightly.

—You follow me?

He turned and limped through the airport. His *songkok*—the black cap that appeared to be worn by all Malay men—was spattered with mold.

A Tamil woman whose raggedy sarong was also badly soiled pushed a wet rag about the airport building floor with a stick. An infant child slept in a cloth tied around her chest. The woman appeared to be immersed in mortification, and would not look up from her task at anyone. There were Malay government officials and Chinese businessmen. The Malays offered smooth pleasantries to each other, while the Chinese hurtled about the room clamoring for attention. Tamil trishaw drivers called out for fares outside the windows, and numerous white soldiers made their way back and forth, their weapons slung over their shoulders. They spoke all sorts of English, from Australia, New Zealand, and Britain, in so many accents that Collins could barely place them at all. Like a great pyramid, the tail of a British army transport plane moved past the window looking out on the tarmac.

Collins had been briefed in Washington on the border war that was being fought at the time between Malaysia and Indonesia. But just now, the war seemed a great deal less important to him than the fresh inundation of rain coming across the runway.

Coconut trees clattered about in the wind, blustery with water. Collins followed Saladin out the exit into the storm. The Malay was headed across the grass toward a Land Rover, weighed down by the American's bags. There was an odor in the air, the same odor that had washed through the plane the moment they had opened the door. It was familiar to Collins, though he could not name it. And now it took him over, wilting him even more as he passed beneath several large palms swirled about by the storm. It was a dark odor, quite sweet, that for the moment superseded the memories of espresso and milk, Lipton Orange Pekoe, Oreo cookies ... all the things Collins's memory had conjured up as he had tried to remember what the odor was. And then he got it. It was that of Lapsang Soochong tea, the same tea he had bought for years in San Francisco from Mr. Yick, who owned a store down the street from his apartment.

—I am assigned to give you a tour of Kuching, Saladin said. Though quite correct, his English had a mechanical feel, as though, in order to speak, Saladin had to turn on a switch.

—Oh, that's all right, Collins replied. —I'm a little tired, to tell you the truth. And wet. Can we go to the hotel? What's its name, the Hotel ...

Saladin threw Collins's bags into the back compartment, then gestured the American toward the rider's side. —A tour is better.

—But ...

—This is the new Malaysia, Saladin continued, jumping into the driver's seat. Water dripped from his *songkok*. He surveyed the steering wheel, as though rehearsing his words. —We live in peace here. All races together, hand to hand. He started the engine, and the Land Rover lurched toward the road leading into town.

They did not go to the hotel. First they went to the Kuching river docks, and Saladin shepherded Collins to a taxi boat for a ride across the river to the *Astana*. The boatman stood at the rear and paddled, chatting with Saladin as they approached the building, a colonial-looking structure with wide porches all around. The grounds were covered with coconut palms.

—It is here that the White Rajahs lived, Saladin said, waiting for Collins to pay the boatman. —As in many places around the world, they were English.

Collins paid, then awaited his change.

—*Terimah kaseh,* the boatman said, thanking Collins. He turned away and set out once more, in a light rain, grateful for the very large tip.

—Their name was Brooke, Saladin continued. —They came in the last century. He made a gesture toward the building.

Collins hurried up the bank after the Malay. —They were ...

—They were fine men, excellent leaders, brave. Rajah James was first, from 1841 to 1868.

—He was born in India, wasn't he? Benares, I think.

—Established head hunting as a capital crime. Saladin lowered his hand and looked up at Collins. —Quite right, don't you think?

—Of course!

—Put down the Chinese opium smugglers.

—Yes, and ...

—Was succeeded by his nephew, Rajah Charles Johnson Brooke. Who was succeeded by *his* son, Sir Charles Vyner Brooke.

Collins gave up. He was not usually such a passive tourist, but he had never been overseas before, and he was uncertain how to act among people who were, essentially, his hosts. Despite his impatience to get to the hotel, he did not want to bully Saladin, as he had imagined the colonialists had. Collins grimaced at the idea of his dispensing orders in British walking shorts. Was he to follow in the footsteps of Chinese Gordon, whose colonial blindness had cost him his life at the hands of the dervishes of Khartoum? Not bloody possible, Collins thought.

Just then he recalled the words of an Englishman who had given an AID seminar on Borneo in Washington. His name was Taylor Curtly, and he had spent some time one afternoon describing for Collins the various peoples in Sarawak. He was under contract from the British Colonial Service, training candidates for State Department positions in former Asian colonies. He was a tall man, with the appearance of a parson, whose schooled accent gave him an air of learned certainty. But Curtly spoke in a tired manner. Indeed, as he went through his characterizations, Collins became exhausted by them.

Taylor held a pinky between the fingers of his other hand. —Chinese? Businesslike. Noisy. Don't much care for the white man. Can't be trusted, of course.

He moved to the ringfinger, and so on to the following fingers as he went down the list.

—Malays? Pliant. Friendly. Lazy. Sikhs? Bloody marvelous doormen and servants. Tamils? Black as can be and unruly. Emotion-laden beggars, the lot of them. And the tribes?

Curtly shook his head, dropping his hands to the table before him. He wore a gray suit, and Collins realized that everything about Curtly was the same color … the suit, his hands, his intonation.

—Savages. You can forget about them altogether, I should think.

—And what about the Brits? Collins had asked. His use of the slang term—its rudeness—surprised him. But he felt that Curtly's descriptions of the people got what strength they had merely from his snide tone. They were devoid of inquiry. Collins wondered whether this tiresomeness in the Englishman came from the rigors of his colonial life or from some more general, inbred emptiness.

—Well, Curtly replied —we ran the place. His eyes lowered toward the table and his shoulders slouched. His gray eyebrows reminded Collins of puffs of cold air. —Didn't we? He appeared suddenly quite stale and unnerved.

Back at the docks, Saladin hired a trishaw. —Excellent transport, he observed as they cycled through another cloudburst. The skin of the driver, a Tamil in a pair of shorts held up with string, glistened with rainwater. —Though these Tamils are very slow, Saladin went on —Chinese much faster.

—You don't say, Collins replied. Though the driver had pulled up the collapsible cover, like the top of an ancient convertible, Collins was once again soaked. Rain fell through a rip in the cover, passed over his shoulders, and rolled down his back.

—But use caution, Saladin mumbled, leaning close to Collins as though to share a secret. —You arrive sooner with the Chinese. But you not careful, you also arrive with less money.

They visited the Sarawak Museum, where Collins studied an exhibit on an Iban longhouse for a moment.

—We must move along, Saladin said.

Then they went to the bus station pavilion for lunch. The trishaw pulled into a space at one end of the station. Buses growled in and out of the curbed lanes, most of them overrun with passengers as they arrived. They were just as laden, with different passengers, when they left.

As Collins got out of the trishaw, he pulled his sunglasses from his bag. Distracted while trying to open them, he stumbled, putting out a hand and catching himself against the building wall.

He had almost fallen over a woman sitting on the sidewalk. She was very old and she was raving. The tattoos on her throat were so gray that they looked like fading shadows, and her sarong was smirched with grease and filth. She took the fingers of his hand. She seemed to look through him, though he knew she was intent on giving him some kind of information. Her voice crackled.

Confused, Collins allowed her to caress his hand. He recognized her tattoos from many of the photos he had seen, realizing that she was an Iban, one of the upriver tribes of which he had read. But she had little of the dignity that the pictures had conveyed. Her anguish was so extreme that she appeared to be obsessed with a kind of skeletal hilarity. She was laughing at him, and Collins smiled back at her. He wondered if he were being cursed. Yet she offered him her hand, and her raving had a genuinely friendly edge, as though she just wished to greet him.

—Come along, Saladin interrupted. He brushed the woman's hand aside, muttering something to her in a language Collins did not understand. —Pay no attention to her. She just here to do you a bad deed.

Collins began to object. The phrase sounded quite intentionally offensive to him. A bad deed? This woman?

Saladin waved his hand. —People like these should go back to the woods. They come to Kuching, but they are no help to the new nation. As he spoke, his eyes narrowed, and his sunglasses did little to hide his nervousness.

—Saladin, she doesn't have any money!

—Please, Mister. Saladin fluttered his hand before Collins's face, then pointed to the end of the building. —Lunch. He pulled Collins away.

A large open plaza beyond the bus station was sheltered by canvas, beneath which there were about a hundred card tables. The cooking area inside was divided into small kitchens, each manned by a Chinese chef working over a burner. Saladin secured one of the empty tables and waited for Collins to order. The menu was written in Chinese characters, and Collins hoped he was not holding it upside down. He looked about at other tables nearby, saw a plate of broccoli and pork in black bean sauce that was being shared by several Chinese, and ordered that. When it was served, Saladin turned his nose up at the food, and moved his chair back from the table a few inches.

In later weeks, Collins would learn that he should not order such a thing in front of a Muslim. But the pork was delicious, and the movements of the Chinese waiters beneath the pavilion attracted his attention. He did not know, at that moment, whether he would ever be able to take in so many details as flooded his view.

He knew he had wanted this, or something like it, this vision that moved in waves before him on his first day in Borneo. Plucked, cooked chickens hung from the outside of the glass cases at each stall. Inside the cases, protected from the numerous flies, were vegetables, sliced pork, peanuts, and chilis of every sort. As rainwater buffeted the canvas above, the shouts of the waiters confused him, as did the spectacle of so many red-skinned English soldiers waiting out the rain with bottles of Tiger Beer, of steam coming up from the shark-fin soup, and of bearded Sikh businessmen in turbans looking like potentates or pashas. The heat embraced Collins. As he ate, his clothes hung with sweat. His shirt held tight to his belly and underarms, as though the perspiration were tar. Saladin accepted a cup of tea from Collins. He muttered at the cracked cup in which the tea was served.

Collins had a cup of coffee himself, and finally the two men returned to the trishaw. The American was tired and exhilarated. He held his shoulder bag close. He needed a shower and a bed.

As he approached the trishaw, he paused to wait for Saladin, who had gone into a shop for some cigarettes. Something touched Collins's hand. The beggar woman had scuttled up the sidewalk toward him and now gripped his pants leg. Her voice rose through a gravelly question and she held her other hand out, palm up. The hand jabbed toward Collins. Her jaw fell open and shut. The words made no sense. They could have been in any language, Collins felt, even English.

—Mister! Saladin pushed the woman's hand aside. Then, to Collins's astonishment, he slapped her. She fell away, apparently unable to stand up. Cowering against the wall, she appeared to shrink, though she continued her mad raving.

—Saladin, what are you doing? Collins said.

Saladin threatened to strike her again. She collapsed to the sidewalk, her soiled hands protecting her head.

—Stop that! Collins shouted.

The Malay's mouth quivered. He folded his hands, which then flew apart again as he struggled to explain himself.

—Tuan, these people shame us.

—*Tuan?* What's that word? Collins could not remember what it signified. He had read it somewhere. It was like mister or something ... as one might say, Mister Englishman.

—Please, Saladin said. —We do not like these beggar people.

—You don't have the right to hit her.

25

The Malay winced with embarrassment. His look at the sidewalk was actually sniveling. —But I'm protecting you, he mumbled.

—Protecting me! Collins replied. —From what? From some harmless ... He looked past Saladin at the madwoman, who remained curled up on the sidewalk. —Some poor, crazy ...

The woman's voice rose up to a cacophony, rattling and certain in its pursuit of Collins. Distracted, the American adjusted his sunglasses.

—What's she saying, anyway?

Forced to listen, Saladin shook his head.

—Something about the forest, he said. He gestured toward the Land Rover. —Please, Tuan, we have to go.

—But what is it?

Again, Saladin cocked his head toward the woman. Her voice cut through the noise of the buses' engines.

—Oh, she is mad, you know. She says the tuans will never understand the forest.

—What forest?

—This forest, Tuan, Saladin replied. He gestured all around him.

—But Kuching's a city.

—Of course, Saladin said quite irritated. —But you step outside Kuching, not far ... He pointed over his shoulder. —A mile from here. Then, you see the forest.

—And she thinks it's dangerous? Collins smiled.

—She thinks if you go out there, Saladin grumbled, embarassed by the admission —maybe you *stay* out there.

—You mean, because I'll like it?

Saladin listened a moment longer.

—That's not what she says, he replied.

—What, then?

—She says you just won't come back.

A group of Malays, on their way to the bus station, stepped

over the woman and passed Collins and Saladin. —Cheerio, John, one of them said, elbowing his friends and laughing.

—Tuan, Saladin said —the Americans told me ...

—What Americans?

—Tuan Jones, the Malay replied. —He works at your consulate. He said to take you around. Saladin wrinkled his nose. —To bring you to this bloody Chinese place. He said all Americans like Chinese food. He said to show you the ropes, and that means ...

—I know what it means.

—Oh. Sorry, Saladin said. He pronounced the words very quickly, as though saying them caused him actual pain.

—Saladin, Collins said. —What does she mean, that I'll never come back?

—Tuan, I'm afraid I'll be sacked if you go round meddling with such as these. Saladin looked over his shoulder again at the woman.

—You won't be sacked. I wouldn't allow that to happen.

Collins pushed roughly past Saladin, who now cowered against the building.

—Oh, Tuan. The Malay's voice descended to a moan. He turned away, his lips drawn down. There was dismay in the sound, as though he had just entered upon personal ruin.

Collins held up and turned back toward the Malay. Suddenly contrite, he realized that he had almost twice the bulk of Saladin. Standing in the middle of the muddy sidewalk, his shoulders enormous, his hands on his waist and his sunglasses glaring down upon the tiny Malay, he felt like a frightening, spectral colonialist.

—So what? he muttered to himself.

He stepped once more toward the woman. Taking her right hand in his, he gripped her fingers. She mumbled in delirium.

—Thank you, Collins said. —Thank you. I'm very glad to be here.

I think I will go see Eddie, Collins said as Joe Salt slung his camera bag over his shoulder. They walked toward the front of the cafe. —I've never been up there to Bintang.

Salt nodded. —You'll like it. The Baleh's a beautiful river, you know. And, like I say, Eddie's the best I've seen.

A shout hurtled through the cafe from the kitchen. It was Ah Woo, who had raised a metal spatula over his head and was yelling at the photographer. He spoke in Malay.

—How about a picture of me, Tuan? he said. He waved the spatula in the air as Collins translated.

—Sure, Salt replied. He pulled his camera from the bag. —Go on over there with him, will you, Dan?

Collins walked to the kitchen—two tables at the back of the cafe, arranged on either side of a single wok over a single gas burner. He put his arm around Ah Woo's shoulder, who raised his spatula once more and, with his free hand,

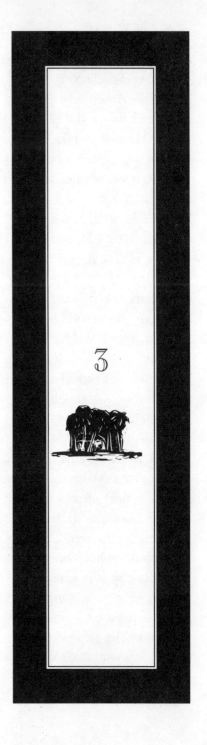

3

gave the thumbs up. Salt snapped the shutter as gravy dripped from the spatula onto Collins's shoulder.

Collins made arrangements for his visit to Eddie Gould and left Kuching a week later. He took a Chinese cargo boat to Kapit, on the Rajang River, then hired a longboat for the trip to Bintang. After three and a half days' travel on the tributary Baleh, his boat reached the first of the river's extensive system of rapids. Salt had mentioned these, and how they formed the beginning of the big forests. The ironwood trees that grew out over the water were held together by the mesh of ferns and deciduous plants that formed a gigantic cliff on each shore. There were several steep rapids through which the boat would have to pass. The boat driver shouted at the guide in the prow, who pointed the way through each plateau of rocks.

As the boat progressed up the river, Collins pondered Eddie's peculiar success.

Eddie was a frail-looking man who seemed to float through his thoughts. His voice was breathy and whimsically monotonous, even on those rare occasions when he told a joke. But he had had all the qualifications the government looked for in an AID official. His engineering degrees were from M.I.T. He had worked for a few years in a firm in Miami as a project engineer for the highway department, for which he had received high commendations. The only negative remark, written by a state functionary, observed that Eddie's silences were peevish and often mocking. —I've noticed that, if he doesn't answer you, he's upset with you, it read. —Also, he can be very forgetful.

Eddie had spent his first weeks of orientation listening to the advice of Collins and the local administrators. In the evenings, he played chess against himself. He had a shelfful of books about chess, whose company he seemed to prefer to that of his colleagues. Eddie liked baseball as well.

—The statistics, actually, he explained to Collins one afternoon, just before going into a short lecture on why no one would ever get as many hits as Ty Cobb. It was, Eddie believed, not possible if you looked at the numbers, and as he explained why, he stared crookedly at Collins, his eyes magnified by the thick lenses of his glasses. His sentences were long and filled with details, numbers, and formulae.

Collins liked baseball, too. But he quickly tired of Eddie's expertise, even though he sensed that the man found solace in such exhaustive precision. The trouble is, Collins observed, you don't dare ask him a question, for fear he'll answer it.

One evening, however, the conversation did not focus on Eddie or his hobbies. To Collins's suprise, it was his fluency in the Iban language that piqued Eddie's interest.

—Can you be fluent, Dan ... I mean truly fluent, if your own life has been led so far from theirs?

—I think so, Collins replied. —Why not?

—Oh, you know, words are just signs pointing out the swamp, see? Eddie adjusted his horn-rims. —They may or may not have blood in them. Dirt. Sweat and shit.

Collins peered into the deep indentations to either side of Eddie's nose.

—But you can't know much about this particular swamp, I'll bet, Eddie continued —if you come from ... where is it you're from? San Francisco?

—That's right, Collins said.

—Yeah, Eddie paused, distracted. —Willie McCovey. He passed a moment in silence, then moved on. —You have to evolve out of the bog to know what the bog really contains. Don't you think? I mean, what do words have to do with that?

For one thing, Collins thought, knowing how to talk to these people might keep you from going screwy. I mean, there's so little to fall back on in a place like this. True, there was the government, the system he and Eddie represented and the employer who paid them. But Washington was fifteen thousand miles away. Its moral pull was therefore weak.

30

As if to underscore that fact, Eddie, so well trained by Washington, so filled up with a battery of State Department certitudes, had abandoned that training immediately.

Eddie's initial assignment had been to supervise the building of a new runway at the Kuching airport. With very little hesitation, he turned it down in favor of going far, far into the outback. Collins, who at the time had just been promoted to run the AID program in Sarawak, remembered his own reluctance to let Eddie do it—a reluctance strengthened by Eddie's youthful arrogance. Eddie seemed to have no consideration for himself. He did not care that he was a dignitary. In support of his petition for a post in the jungle, he argued that if everyone were aware of the consequences of their actions, no one would ever do anything.

So, finally, Eddie ascended the Baleh River, much farther than even the Malaysian government had thought advisable. So few Ibans lived in Bintang that it was unthinkable that any foreigner would wish to go there. None ever had. But Eddie seemed to feel that there was no reason to do any of this if he did not immerse himself in it totally.

After he had gone up the river, there had been no word from him for six months. He was supposed to be mapping the uncharted tributary streams of the Baleh, and Collins assumed that he was doing so. When Eddie finally came down to the division capital of Kanowit to pick up his mail, Collins was there to see him. They spent an afternoon together talking about work. Eddie spoke with enthusiasm about the traveling he had done and about how valuable the upriver Ibans were to his mapping.

—They take you places you can't imagine, Dan, he had said, pushing his glasses up the bridge of his nose. He spoke in a manner that was altogether professional, Collins thought. Wordy information, exhaustively cataloged. He hadn't changed. Reassured that Eddie was merely a fervid civil servant, not harmful or nuts, Collins let him return upriver, where he continued working for another year.

Now, the forest formed a long, sun-dappled cavern about Collins's boat as he made his way to visit Eddie. He was certain they would arrive at the upper rapids at Rumah Bintang before noon. The river narrowed considerably, and the forest grew darker. The trees were very thick; their variegated roots gripped the banks like broken hands. There were fewer people, but, if anything, the atmosphere was friendlier with the wet odors of fruit and fallen green. The river was very clear.

The boat ascended steep rapids that were quite extensive, a barrier to most travel farther upriver. It paused periodically in its ascent, then turned and scurried loudly through each portal of white water. At the top, on the right bank opposite two large boulders through which the entire river passed in violent falls, the longhouse Rumah Bintang jutted from the forest.

The house was so successfully hidden by the jungle that its size was difficult to judge. Collins saw only the end of it that contained the main door, at the top of a notched log that formed the stairway. The house appeared to lean out over the river, high up above the water, on top of a rise.

The entire structure was ten feet above the forest floor, built on hundreds of hardwood pilings. Collins knew that the house extended back into the forest. But here the forest itself was a curtain of ferns and trees, so interwoven and messy that the sunlight could barely make its way through. The one feature of the house that made it stand out from the jungle was its color, that of years-old thatch. Gray and darker gray, it was like a fallen tree.

The driver moored the boat opposite the falls, and Collins walked up a path toward the longhouse. Several hundred Ibans had gathered on the boulders overlooking the river. They now descended to the bank, and Collins saw there was a long gauntlet of women leading to the longhouse, each holding a palm frond extended into the air. The pathway between the women led to the notched log. A middle-aged Iban man, grizzled and brown in a black loincloth, his mouth obscured by an enormous home-made cigar, walked down from the house with three other Ibans to greet Collins. The Iban had to shout to be heard over the roar of the falls.

—Good afternoon, Tuan, he said.

It was difficult at first for Collins to understand the man's spoken Iban, since his mouth was filled with spittle, brought on by a large chunk of betel nut.

—Thank you for coming. I am Headman Lupit.

He stepped forward and shook Collins's hand, once. He leaned to the side and spat onto the ground.

—We're honored by your visit, he said.

Lupit gestured to the other men, who Collins realized were chiefs of other houses farther upriver. The Ibans must have heard of his coming and prepared for this moment. He had often been feted during his travels around the country and had never learned how information passed so quickly up and down the rivers. The men offered him cigarettes and a small glass of *tuak* wine. Collins quickly downed it. He looked toward the longhouse.

—May I speak with Eddie? he asked in Iban.

Lupit gestured toward the women. Collins walked up the path beneath the raised fronds. There were expressions of wonder. Collins's appearance this deep in the jungle proved Tuan Eddie was a weighty personage, very important to the White Man's Way. Surely now their forest was blessed. The crop would do well. Great fortune had come upon them.

Several children broke from the surrounding crowd to scurry toward the longhouse. But their clamor, each child vying to enter the house first, was interrupted by the appearance in the doorway of Tuan Eddie himself—a great bird, Collins thought—a mannered, gorgeous apparition.

He was dressed in a black loincloth. His body was tattooed, everywhere, in geometric designs and figures of birds and snakes.

The tattoos were similar to those Collins had seen on numerous chieftains up and down the rivers. But they were far more stylized and fluid. There was writing on some of them as well. *Get off my cloud,* in blue, etched across one shoulder. *I can't get no satisfaction* on one leg. Collins realized the tattoos were of Eddie's own design. He saw that they were made from charcoal and local dyes and were therefore temporary. The beak of a bird's head, drawn across his throat, was smeared.

Eddie's elaborate tribal appearance made his white skin seem incongruous. He resembled an emaciated ghost, done up artfully. His glasses, askew on his face, gave him a comic, priestly look. One lens was cracked, and a stem was held to the rest of the frame with soiled white adhesive tape.

Eddie's headdress alarmed Collins. Numerous long feathers, blue and green, appeared to leap from the band that held them to his head. As he lowered himself step by step, the feathers jostled each other in the air. The headdress was not a traditional one. Collins had never seen one like it, and he guessed it too had been made by Tuan Eddie. The feathers were like small leaves rustling against one another, their delicacy posing a contrast to the rugged noise of the river.

—Hello, Dan, Eddie said. He extended his hand. His face was barely lined. —I'm very glad you've come up to see us.

He spoke in Iban. The small patches of fluff on Eddie's chin had been there several weeks, Collins guessed, but they were not yet a beard.

—What the hell is all this? Collins asked. His reply, in English, seemed to intimidate Eddie, who immediately broke into English himself.

—All what?

—This playacting. The feathers. What are you doing up here?

Eddie remained silent a moment. At first he appeared confused. He dropped his hand.

—What's going on? Collins asked.

Eddie looked down at the tattoos on his body. —Nothing's going on. I thought you'd like all this stuff. That's why I wore it.

Collins's heart battered inside him, and at first he could not understand the violence of his reaction. There was comedy in Eddie's appearance, but the comedy offended Collins because, he feared, it put Eddie in considerable jeopardy. Not with the Ibans. Rather, he worried about how such behavior would be viewed in Washington. Is this what Joe Salt photographed? Collins placed his hands on his waist and looked down at the mud. Is this what the American public will see?

Eddie held out his hand once more. —It's great to see you, he offered.

The crowd of Ibans had gathered around them. Each of the men wore a loincloth similar to Eddie's, and their bodies were tattooed in dark blue. The men wore their hair quite long in a traditional cut that exposed their ears. Many of them had long, pierced ear-lobes that extended below their jaws. The women, bare-breasted, wore black cotton sarongs about their waists. One of them stood to one side behind Eddie, very young and very shy.

She's no more than thirteen, Collins thought. She stared at the ground, then glanced at the two white men. There was a smile on her lips. Her hands and feet had the same thickness as those of the other women, which came from the difficult work they did, the exposure to the sun and mud. But she was the daughter of a wealthy tribesman, Collins thought, judging from the heavy brass rings that hung from each earlobe. The rings were a fash-ionable adornment that Collins found attractive in the Iban women. The balance required to keep them from swinging about gave the women a very correct posture and a careful step. So small, they walked with extreme delicacy despite the obvious difficulties they faced in their lives in the forest.

Eddie noticed Collins's interest.

—This is Lama, he said. —My wife.

This news of Eddie's wife dismayed Collins. —We've heard

quite a bit about you downriver, Eddie. And I want to talk with you about it ... in private.

Eddie laughed. —But nobody here can speak English, Dan.

Collins looked about at the Ibans. The Americans, white-skinned and fleshy, were a foot taller than any of the natives. The Ibans, dignified in their grubbiness, stood very respectfully at a distance. A pall of smoke from their homemade cigarettes hung over the group.

—I want to be alone anyway, Collins said.

—Oh, all right, Eddie replied. —Come on, we'll take a walk up the river.

He asked the Ibans to leave them alone a while. Collins, sensing Lupit could be offended, addressed him.

—Excuse us, he said in Iban. —I'm honored to be here, and thank you for your kindness. We are old friends and wish just a moment of privacy.

The headman nodded and turned away, gesturing the others back to the longhouse.

The two Americans walked along the riverbank above the falls. They entered a shady area beneath several large trees. Collins leaned against one of the trees and folded his arms. Eddie, his feathers waffling about on a breeze, hunkered down like an Iban tribesman, hands hanging listlessly about his knees. The posture seemed to Collins phony, mannered, as though Eddie wished to show some kind of cultural superiority to the other American.

—So you put on this outfit just for me? Collins asked.

—No, Eddie smiled. —I dress this way all the time.

Collins closed his eyes and remained silent a moment. —Why, Eddie?

—Because they do. Eddie picked up a pebble from the ground and tossed it listlessly toward a tree several feet away.

Collins became outraged. —I want you out of here, he said.

—But why? Eddie replied. He wiped his shoulder, and a portion of the tattoo smeared beneath his hand.

—We're in a delicate position, Eddie. You represent the U.S. State Department, you know, and as such ...

—That's right, Eddie interrupted. —That's the way I feel about it.

Collins sighed. He was anxious to say everything he could as quickly as possible. The weight of his task, so large and with so little time to consider it, seemed to blurt from him all at once. Eddie had sold himself into primitive, irrational debauchery, and he proved it with his tattoos, with the grandiose idiocy of his feathers.

—I do! Eddie continued. —I came up here and did what I was supposed to do.

—What? Become an Iban?

Eddie looked down at his feet. —No. I've taught these people how to grow green beans. You know what that means? They've got greens in their diet. First time ever. That's what I'm talking about. And we got them some chickens.

—Oh, I know all about that, Collins interrupted. —Don't talk to me about chickens.

—But that's what I'm supposed to do, isn't it, Dan?

—What?

—Help out. I was trained to come out here and do this. I was trained! By you! Eddie pursed his lips, and his eyes tightened as if he were caught in a deception. —To befriend the people. That's what you told us to do. Show them how good the Americans are.

—But not like this! Collins shouted. His exasperation startled Eddie, who actually began to pout. His headdress fluttered again in the warm breeze. Collins noticed the group of Ibans far below and was surprised by the number that remained outside the longhouse. Virtually the entire village stood before the house, watching the Americans with marked intent. There was a stoic mournfulness about them.

A white parabola of mist rose up through the forest. Inundated with water, the ground glistened. The forest seemed gloomy,

37

heavy, yet it was speckled with wild fruits and orchids. Collins felt a kind of comfort from it. It was obscure, yet at the same time it had a dark lilt, a darkness of exceeding beauty. It carried an atmosphere of sweat.

Collins's own work with the Ibans had been conducted far downriver in peopled farmlands, where the British had been for a century. He knew the Ibans. They marveled at his ability to speak their language. But Collins had seldom seen anything like this. He imagined his own enjoyment of the place, living in such forceful fruition.

—Do you know what this is going to look like? Collins asked. —How the people in Washington are going to feel about this?

—Who cares? How are they going ...

—You're going to be famous, Eddie. Collins's repetition of Joe Salt's words caused him to shudder. He imagined the State Department ... Dean Rusk himself, probably, thumbing through the latest issue of *National Geographic,* coming across Eddie as he hunkered on the longhouse porch polishing his blowgun or weaving a basket or some other damned thing. —Who runs that show out there? Rusk would ask, and the assistant would find out that it was Dan Collins who ran that show.

—Famous? Eddie asked.

—Yes. That *Geographic* article.

Eddie grimaced. —Dan. Pardon me, he said. —But I think you're being foolish.

Collins moved a few feet from the tree. He looked down at Eddie, who remained squatting on the ground. The look on Eddie's face, a kind of lackadaisical pity, caused Collins to want to knock the feathers from his head.

—Goddamn you ...

—Look, I'm going down to the longhouse to ask Lama to make us some lunch, Eddie said. He stood and turned down the trail. As Eddie jumped over a large root, Collins noticed the soles of his feet had hardened and cracked, and that they appeared to have spread out, like those of the Ibans themselves.

—Secure your boat, Eddie said as he retreated —and come have something to eat. We can settle this pretty easily.

A half hour later Collins entered the longhouse and walked the length of the porch toward Eddie's room. The floor was made of bamboo slats, and his passage caused a clatter that startled the animals below. The house had seventy-five rooms side by side, each of which fronted on the porch. Collins acknowledged the greetings offered by the Ibans who worked there. Though it was still daytime, the light that entered through the doors from the outer porch did little to push back the gloom. Collins paused a moment to speak with a woman who wove a large rice basket. She sat in a swatch of sun near a door. Her thick fingers pushed the rattan straw in and out of the basket frame. Her hair, which was graying, was pulled back into a tight bun. She wore a sarong about her waist. Her left foot lay on its side where it extended from beneath the sarong.

—How long does a basket like this last? Collins asked.

The woman did not look up at him, and replied with an indifferent tone that sounded insulting. Collins knew, however, from his own work with the Ibans that she was simply shy and reticent. She continued the work as she spoke.

—Many years, Tuan. The only problem is that we can't keep the rats away.

—The basket's large, Collins said.

—Yes, she replied. —A year's worth of rice. The rats can eat a month's worth, so it's important we keep them out.

Collins smiled and pointed toward the far end of the house.

—Is Tuan Eddie's room down there?

—Yes, it's the next to last, next to the headman's.

Collins thanked her. When he entered the room, he saw Eddie seated at the rear next to the folded mat that served as his bed. He was repairing a basket, and as Collins approached, he gestured toward a mat next to him.

—Looks like you're enjoying yourself up here, Eddie.

Eddie's face retained a childish puffiness, though Collins realized he had lost quite a bit of weight. He wondered if Eddie were not enacting a youthful ideal—that he'd become, through some insanity, an innocent in the forest. In other cases like this of which he had heard, Collins suspected something destructive—that the person was involved in escape, that the isolation and the jungle became, bad as they were, preferable to whatever that person had left. Such people went native with a scowl and made of their effort a self-righteous cause. But Eddie seemed gewgawed, humorous. He's like a kid, Collins thought. Can't judge. His innocence has put him in this damned loincloth. He'll be insulted when I tell him to put on his pants.

—I'm interested in the tattoos, Eddie.

—You like them? I made them myself, Eddie said as he surveyed the bird on his chest. —They're like Lupit's—my father-in-law, Dan. Eddie chuckled a moment. —I should tell you, he continued. —I've become ... well, a kind of prime minister to him. Vice-chief, I guess.

—What do you mean, you're a king or something?

—No, no. Just second in command, I suppose. Incognito, though. Incognito.

Collins looked over the tattoos on Eddie's arm. They were badly smeared, and when he touched one of them, the dye came off on his fingers. A tin pot fell to the floor of the cubicle at the rear of the room, and a woman peered around the bamboo partition. It was Lama, who giggled as she walked into the room.

—Excuse me, she said. —The fire's hot.

Lama spoke with a fine accent. Her face, which carried little worry, appeared so fresh that she made Collins smile.

—So, what do you think these people are? Eddie blurted as he pushed the steel needle through the basket. Lama, embarrassed and pleased by Collins's visit, returned to the kitchen. —Why do they frighten you?

—They don't frighten me, Collins replied.

—Then what do you have against loincloths or tattoos? Or my feathers?

As he asked these questions, Eddie became noticeably angry. He hunched his shoulders forward to listen.

—But, Eddie, it's not their customs I'm against. It's yours!

Eddie set the basket and needle down. —For what reason could you be offended by them?

Collins wondered whether Eddie were not having fun with this. The drama of the conversation seemed to enliven him, while it merely irritated Collins, who felt there really should be no question of the impropriety of Eddie's actions.

—Here's the issue, Eddie. We have rules. I mean, the State Department has. It causes political problems when our people decide to go native. Malaysian government doesn't like it. It looks bad for them because they have to admit they have natives.

Collins grinned.

—Our government doesn't like it because ... well, we represent the way it's supposed to be, you know. American technology, progress ...

As he made his way through his explanation, Collins began to feel himself wandering. The words had the ring of patriotism, but it was a rehearsed patriotism. Frankly, they sounded to Collins like the advice of a team player, a party hack. He felt ridiculous. Eddie leaned back against the wall. He raised his knees and let his hands rest on them. The fingers were quite soiled, the nails cracked. But, Collins thought, ridiculous or not, what I'm saying carries weight. There is bureaucratic punishment involved here. He imagined how Eddie would be treated if someone came from Washington to ferret out what was really happening. Party hacks, yes, Collins thought. But he knew the wrath just the sight of Eddie in his feathers would engender. So he pressed on.

—Look, Collins continued. —No matter what happens to our people out here, no matter how ... democratic you may feel, there's one thing you can't do.

—What's that?

—Become one of them. You know, an Iban. Or a Swahili. Or an Untouchable. Doesn't matter who the host population is.

—The natives, you mean.

—Right, damn it. The natives. It doesn't matter what else you do. You just don't do that. State Department rule number one.

—Why not? Eddie asked.

—The governments are offended. And if you have a government that's offended ...

—Oh, fuck your governments.

Eddie examined his fingers a moment. His insult seemed to have calmed him.

—Because there *is* something better, Dan, he said. —In the jungle.

—How?

—Something that puts an end to all that. He took the needle into his hand once more. —I've always thought I could find something like this, you know. I came out here looking for it.

—Now, I know that. Now, I can see it. But ...

—The way the forest is so crazy here. Have you looked at it?

—Of course I have, Eddie.

—The way it wanders in itself, intertwined like that. Or the sounds. The way the birds.... Or the monsoon. Have you seen it when it washes over everything?

— Sure, I ...

—What does rain like that mean to you? What does it mean, such lightning?

Alarmed, Collins now imagined the Minister of the Interior for Malaysia, Datu Zainal Ibrahim, who spoke perfect Oxford English, chiding him for the unseemly spectacle of an American living like, well, like Tarzan, Mr. Collins. Altogether unacceptable. And in the pages of an international magazine. Awful, Mr. Collins. Really quite awful.

—I've got to implore you, Eddie. Give this up. Come back downriver with me. This here ... Collins pointed at the basket, then looked about the room. —You can't do this.

He stood and moved toward the door. Lama looked around the edge of the partition. When she saw Collins was leaving, she glanced at Eddie, who silently remained seated on the floor.

—You're not staying? she asked.

Collins attempted a smile, then shook his head. He addressed Eddie in English.

—I don't see how I can stay, Eddie. I'm proposing something to you that you obviously don't want to do. I guess I'm the enemy, really.

—Sure, if you wish, Eddie replied. —But you're my guest. Lama's made a lunch for us.

Collins opened the door. He was struck by the sad look of surprise on Lama's face.

—I'm sorry, Eddie. We've got to go tomorrow. I want you to go with me.

He closed the door behind him and walked from the longhouse.

Headman Lupit asked Collins to spend the night in his room, and, after an embarrassing ceremony on the porch at which Collins was congratulated for being such a fine man and was told that Eddie was more than just a white man, rather an *orang pandai*—a wise man of great judgment, kindness, and conciliation —Collins slipped away and went to bed. In Lupit's bed, as it happened. The headman himself and his wife slept on the floor.

It began raining, and soon the forest was awash with the storm. The roof thatch absorbed the sound of the rain and deepened it, so that as Collins fell into his uncomfortable sleep, came out of it, and returned, the rain intruded on him like waves up and back on a beach. He rose once and looked out the open window behind the kitchen. The trees blew about with abandon, slick with dark water.

The next morning Collins arranged his gear in the boat. The sun had risen from a gray mist that dispersed into the forest. It was exceedingly warm, and his movements were listless, without

43

spirit. He sat on the bank watching the falls as they split the two boulders above. The mist ascended into the trees and enveloped the lower branches.

Eddie walked down from the house, gesturing at the children who attempted to follow him. They returned to the overlook above, where Collins noticed all the villagers were standing. Eddie's tattoos were now badly smeared, though he still wore his headdress. Collins saw that he had not slept. His eyes were blotched red and unfocused.

—Dan, I'm not leaving, he said.

—Why not?

—My whole family's here. This is what I want. It's too important.

Collins tossed a rock into the river. He did not want to look at Eddie. He wavered at the intensity of the man's distress, and finally he spoke with abrupt rudeness.

—Eddie, get your gear. Now. We're leaving in half an hour.

Eddie swore and turned toward the longhouse. He approached Lupit and Lama and spoke briefly. There then was a long conversation, during which the Ibans grew agitated. They began yelling, gesturing angrily at Collins. Eddie appeared surprised by their response. He shook his head and held his hands out toward them. They pushed him aside and moved down the bank toward Collins.

They looked ready for a battle. Their voices were garbled. They raged through the forest. At first Collins laughed. The matter seemed still to be private, something between the two Americans alone. But then he realized that neither he nor Eddie had seriously inquired about their interests. Suddenly he noticed that one of them was carrying a shotgun. A few were even armed with ancient blowguns. Collins could not imagine them using the weapons. The Ibans were no longer fierce. The last heads had been taken in 1945, and those were from the Japanese, who were true enemies, hardly nervous bureaucrats like Collins himself.

But his fear intensified as he imagined his own head, with a grimacing smile, hilarious, hanging in a basket from the ridgepole of the longhouse.

The forest gathered up behind the Ibans, beyond the long reach of the longhouse, into a kind of gargantuan wall. Such light as there was was muted and gray. The natives now began running toward Collins. Spittle turned acrid in his mouth. He hated his own sense of duty and the cavalier authority he had felt over Eddie's life. Now I'm going to get killed for it, he thought.

Collins spotted Eddie at the rear of the crowd of Ibans. His feathers jounced about his head. He stumbled behind them, shouting. The Ibans approached and began a chant, translated approximately, Collins noticed, as —Yankee go home! over and over again. They waved their blowguns in the air and menaced the American with *parang* knives. Eddie pushed through the crowd. He glowered at Collins as he spoke in Iban.

—Look, you've got to get out of here, he said.

—I know it, but ...

—Do it somehow. I'm sorry this has happened, Dan.

Eddie turned to the Ibans.

—Please, my friends. Thank you for helping me. Go back to the longhouse, please.

He turned again to Collins. —They're angry, Dan, he said in English. —I don't think we can get out of here, no matter what.

Collins, his voice fluttering, pursed his lips.

—Got to, Eddie.

—Oh, Christ! Eddie yelled. —Give this up, would you?

—Now, Eddie. Get your gear now. Take them back to the longhouse with you, and don't bring them back.

—Dan! Eddie shouted. It was not defiance. Collins heard, for the first time, anguish in Eddie's voice. His soiled skin and the feathers, wavering above the crooked glasses on his nose, now became a picture of extreme sadness.

Collins spoke up quickly. —This is important, he yelled. —Just get your clothes, your books, whatever. You're getting out of here.

He turned angrily and walked up the bank, directly below the falls. He sat down on a large boulder shaded by the forest and watched Eddie, followed by the still smoldering crowd of Ibans, as he returned to the longhouse.

Collins wondered what, in all this, he was missing. What had Eddie really done? Am I looking at a case of simple childishness? He surveyed the swirl of the forest, how the mist settled between the trees like a light, shredded fog. Or is Eddie overcome by some kind of dark disintegration, fueled by past angers? His father telling him to shape up, to be more of a man, to get his nose out of those math books. Collins sighed, tossing a rock down the path. How could he, in these few minutes, discover the fumes that had sickened Eddie? How explain them to him?

Or was it romance? Finally in his life, romance, the dark jungle and the spirits turning his head. Lost up the humid river, had Eddie found the alternative that chess and baseball had never provided for him? Had the kite bird warrior spirit reached down from the next world and enflamed his senses?

Collins grumbled at himself, suspecting that these questions were just useless platitudes. Dream platitudes that he himself had fashioned looking out into the jungle for the last five years. Romantic gush. The truth was that these people were poor, their lives a daily scramble in the forest for a little food. Their days were cluttered with death, malnutrition, malaria.

No. It's none of that, Collins thought. He swore darkly at himself as it came to him that there was really little to explain. Eddie's just in love, that's all—in love with his young wife, with the people in upriver Bintang, the forest itself. Eddie had lost his mind. Yet, against his better judgment Collins grudgingly admired the loss. Eddie was a fool. He was a kind of traitor. But this foolishness and treason had been matters of profound feeling, of an admirable sensitivity to beauty, to flesh and fine mud, to the forest. The dilapidated longhouse that seemed always to tilt no matter the perspective, the poverty of the Ibans ... all this simply added to the eeriness of the place. Despite his wish to do so, Collins could come up with nothing to explain it away. Narrowed by his own task, blind to such gorgeous detail, he realized nonetheless that he was destroying Eddie's new life, all for the sake of the bureaucracy and of what was expected of him by Washington. He resented his task. He had brought great power to bear against the powerless. Eddie was right. You are just an intruder.

As he glanced again toward the falls, he saw Lama ascending the path from the longhouse. She walked very carefully, upright. Her negotiation of the rocks, over which she tiptoed while supporting her heavy earrings in the palms of her hands, was quite careful. She glanced at Collins with annoyance, he sensed. After a moment, he realized she was mortified. She approached him, and, very nervous, he stood to greet her.

—I'm sorry, Lama, he said.

—Excuse me, Tuan, I shouldn't do this, but may I plead for Eddie?

—Plead?

—Yes, Lama continued. —Please don't take him away. This is very bad. He's my husband and I love him.

—I ...

—I'll die, Tuan.

—What do you mean?

—My people will reject me if he goes. I can't go with him, and I'll be alone. They'll laugh at me. *Tuan's wife*, they'll call me. *Butterfly*. Make fun of me.

Collins knew how bad this would be for her. *Butterfly* was what the Ibans called a whore. He knew there were many Iban women Lama's age who had already had children of their own. But Lama's appearance defied that possibility. She was tiny. Her eyes glistened. Her shoulders and torso were quite smooth, her dark skin devoid of tattoos, which gave way at her hands to cracked and work-thickened fingers. She looked shamed, like a guilty child.

—You know I can't allow him to stay.

—My father will suffer as well. Lama pointed toward the long-house. —Eddie is his son. He has taught Eddie.

She began weeping. Her tears, heavy and invasive, immediately ruined Collins's protest. He was confused, unable to move.

—What harm is he doing? Lama suddenly asked. Her voice, without control, had risen to a shout.

There was noise from the longhouse. Eddie, dressed in a pair of shorts and a white T-shirt, carried a military duffel on one shoulder. He remained barefoot. He had washed the tattoos from his arms and shoulders, but Collins saw that the dyes had not come away completely. He was followed by a crowd of two hundred Ibans. The talk was chaotic, a rubble of confused protest.

—This is a terrible mistake, Lama muttered.

She turned toward Eddie. Her face was smirched by her tears. When Eddie saw her, he gripped the duffel tightly. He appeared threatened by her grief. He was embarrassed, the way a teenager at a prom would be. There was no embrace.

Lupit led the way ahead of the other Ibans. He walked with a kind of ceremonial heaviness, and Collins realized Lupit was shielding his own unhappiness behind his stoic passage down the pathway. The old man barely looked at Collins, who now turned down the trail toward the boat. Collins did not speak. His descent to the river held no sense of victory for him.

Eddie walked to the boat and threw his duffel into the prow. He did not look back at the bank. He began climbing into the boat when Collins took his arm.

—Look, I can't stand doing it this way, Eddie, he said.

—I'm sorry?

—It's dereliction, Collins continued —the worst sort of dereliction … He glanced at Eddie, then placed his hands in his pockets and glared at the mud below —but you're staying, he finished.

Eddie, distracted by his effort to get into the boat, did not hear. He continued protesting. Collins climbed into the boat.

—I said you're not leaving.

Eddie's face maintained a look of blank misunderstanding.

—Get your gear out of the boat, Collins said.

—But, Dan …

—Please, Collins insisted. —Now. No explanations. No questions.

Confused, Eddie grabbed his duffel and passed it up to the bank. He climbed the bank himself, then stood to watch Collins. Irritated by his own fecklessness, Collins sensed a smile on Eddie's face.

—Three days up here, Collins muttered grumpily. —Just to find out you're doing the right thing. And now three days back.

He motioned to the driver, who engaged the engine. The boat turned about before the falls. Eddie walked up the bank and spoke with Lupit, after which the Ibans broke into immediate raucous noise. Collins could hear none of the celebration because of the roar of the water. Several Ibans ran across the rocks shouting at the boat. Caught a moment in a large riffle before the falls, Collins barely noticed them. They appeared shrouded in the spray up above. After a moment he saw Lupit walking rapidly down the pathway to the edge of the pool. He ordered the driver to return to the bank. As they approached him, Lupit raised his hand into the air. In the sunlit mist his body looked shrunken, like old wood. There was a flurry of color in his hand, Eddie's feathers.

When the boat nudged the shore, Lupit waded into the pool and handed the feathers to Collins.

—Thank you, Tuan, he said. —Please, take them as a gift. For your kindness.

His face, shining with water from the mist, appeared flushed. Collins himself was quite wet, and Lupit placed a hand on his shoulder.

—It's a gift, Lupit shouted.

—For what? For Eddie?

Lupit did not answer. Rather he thrust the feathers onto Collins's head. Collins, disgruntled, adjusted the headdress. Lupit clapped him again on the shoulder.

—Feel damned foolish, Collins grumbled in English.

The boat pulled away from the shore. Caught in the rush of air from the waterfall, the feathers battered Collins's face. He wondered how he would report this to the AID people in Kuala Lumpur. Well, he didn't have to report it. But then there was the article. What'll they do when Salt's article—goddamned Joe Salt, he muttered—comes out? Eddie gone native. Eddie tattooed. Eddie the headhunter. Collins allowed his fears to overtake him entirely, and he slouched against his gear. The boat was lost a moment in the sun-dazzled mist, then moved farther downriver toward the protective isolation of the rapids.

50 Collins sat up and turned to look once again at the Ibans. He glowered at them as they stood on the banks waving. Then he glowered at Eddie who, followed by his wife, shouldered his duffel happily up the notched log into the longhouse, and finally at Lupit, grateful and stoic on the lower shore.

Collins leaned far back against his gear and surveyed the forest as it passed above the boat. The feathers obscured his sight. Maybe he'd wear them when he submitted his report to the people in Kuala Lumpur. He laced his fingers behind his head and sighed in the dappled light. The feathers looked ridiculous on him. Yet, for the moment, he felt they must adorn him, too, as they would a king.

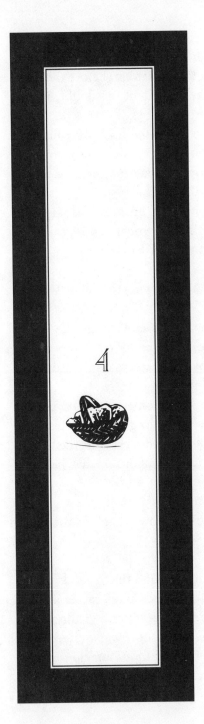

4

John Bull Porvaikkiperunarkilli brought Collins a dinner of fish curry with steamed rice and vegetables, and a bottle of beer. This time Collins was alone in the dining room of His Majesty's Arms. He sat at a corner table facing the entry, so that he would be able to see anyone who came in.

He imagined with considerable pain the State Department's abduction of Eddie Gould from the forest. The Ibans would not realize what it was that was taking him away. Surely the other Americans would appear just as human as Eddie, just as pasty-white and ludicrous. Even kindly, probably. But the true explanation, that Eddie was being kidnapped by a blind bureaucracy, would be meaningless to the Ibans.

—What's a bureaucrat? they would ask.

Outraged in the disappearing light of the afternoon, the forest at their back like a threatening dream filled with serpents and dripping trees, they would be left with no explanation at all.

—'Terminated,' Tuan? What's 'terminated?'

He recalled that Tully Spencer had told him over the radio-telephone that Feeney would try to contact him before the hearing. —He wants to give you the benefit of the doubt, Dan. I mean, you are in charge over there.

Collins had ground the cigarette into the floor with his foot, immediately taking out another. Again the Malay lit it for him. This time Collins gave the pack to the Malay and gestured to him to offer cigarettes to everyone in the office.

—Basically this is Ed Gould's problem, Spencer had said. The telephone hurt Collins's ear. —It's not yours. Though maybe there was a lapse of judgment on your part.

—Of what?

—Judgment. You know that. You're with the State Department, right?

The Malay studied the pack as he moved through the room. Evidently he had never seen Lucky Strikes before. He passed it around, so that others could enjoy the graphics on the front and the protective cellophane wrapping.

—It's not like the Peace Corps, Dan. Some kind of do-gooder out there. He's not a missionary volunteering his soul. This guy's supposed to be the real thing. Eddie Gould represents the United States government. That's why it's so important that he dress right.

—Tully.

—That he look like an American. Know what he's there for.

—Listen …

—And not go crazy.

After dinner, Collins took a stroll around the grounds of His Majesty's Arms. They were hardly grounds at all, rather a patch of thick grass and seven palm trees corraled within a Victorian iron fence, the river just beyond. The half-moon was quite bright, though just now it was being overrun by monsoon clouds coming up the river. The fronds above began to clatter in the fresh wind.

Feeney had made no appearance that evening, and Collins felt like a fool for having been so concerned. Tomorrow, he thought, Eddie will explain himself during the meeting, simple as that, and I'll tell them how it was that Eddie was doing such a good job up there. And then I'll tell Feeney that he shouldn't attach such importance to a frivolous cover photo and article in a decorative, shallow magazine read fervently by ... by how many? By millions of American voters?

By the Secretary of State.

By Leonid Brezhnev.

By the President.

Collins swore and turned back toward the hotel.

The following morning, John brought an envelope to Collins at breakfast. A bright, hot fog had settled on the river, and the hotel was immersed in it. Descending the stairs a few minutes earlier, Collins had noticed John and the rest of the staff standing in the front entry, looking out into the blank mist.

—An American was here this morning, Mister, John muttered secretively, reaching into his pocket. He looked over his shoulder. —He left this for you.

Collins opened the envelope as John poured fresh coffee that was thick with condensed milk and sugar. John glanced toward the entry.

—I told him you were out for a brisk morning *jalan*, he whispered, using the Malay word for "stroll."

—Thanks.

The note was handwritten—hurriedly—by Tully Spencer. The meeting would take place at the American consulate at eleven o'clock that morning. —Be there, it concluded.

Collins stuffed the note into a shirt pocket. —Jesus, he whispered.

—Good news, then? John asked.

Collins went back to his room to dress for the meeting. Realizing that there would be a certain decorum to it, he had packed a tie, a short-sleeved white dress shirt, a leather belt, and a pair of tan slacks. The slacks had been hanging from a hook at the back of his closet for five years, so they were dotted with mold. On the whole, however, he thought he looked presentable, the way he had looked the day he arrived in Sarawak.

When he entered the consul's office, the Malay receptionist gestured across the room.

—Just take a seat there, please, she said. The brown chair leather was quite cold, like oilcloth that had been left out in the snow. Looking about him, Collins discovered he was in a breeze coming down from an air-conditioning grate in the ceiling. Tully Spencer walked into the room.

Spencer had been Collins's boss for two years. Early in their relationship, Collins had stopped telling Spencer about any special projects he had in mind for AID people in Sarawak. A voluntary, casual mention of anything to Spencer caused a storm of official suggestions, with letters back and forth between Kuching and Kuala Lumpur, triplicate forms, requests to Washington. Collins, driven crazy, had decided silence was a better ploy. It was a matter of getting on with things.

Spencer was an overweight man of about fifty. He wore horn-rimmed glasses that sat, very squarely, on his face, and his red hair was combed straight back from his brow. A thick veneer of good humor obscured a cheerless personality. He enjoyed being what he called "an old Asia hand," but his insistence on everything being in writing, approved by higher-ups, and properly signed-off on made that offhand term a sham. Spencer did not truly laugh—he guffawed, but only at things that, for everyone else, were trifles.

Occasionally Spencer had asked if he could travel upcountry with Collins to visit the Americans working there. He enjoyed the junkets. Bad food thrilled him because he thought it so adventuresome. And he asked every sort of question about the beliefs of the natives, puzzling even Collins, who was a kind of authority on the Ibans.

The head-hunting was especially appealing to Spencer, because it was so savage and odd. —An unexplainable custom, dammit, he had said to Collins during a tour of a longhouse once, going on to say that Borneo was certainly one hell of a long way from Dartmouth. The two men were being shown about by an Iban named Robert Dalat, a civil servant from Kuching who had invited them to his longhouse in upriver Paku.

—The interesting thing about the head-hunting is that it was a sign of high civilization, Collins replied.

—How do you figure?

—Head-hunting is risky, of course, Collins shrugged.

—I imagine so.

—And taking that risk meant that a man was a credit to his house. High bravery.

Spencer shivered, his sunburned face tight with disapproval.

—And the thing is, Collins continued, —the best kind of head to get was that of a baby.

—What?

—It's true! A baby would never be out wandering in the woods, see. He would always be at home, inside the longhouse. So to get a baby's head meant that you had to sneak into the enemy house, into the inner sanctum, you might say. Doing that, and coming back with the prize …

Shocked, Spencer looked down at Robert Dalat, who had been listening. Robert nodded, anxious to please the tuan from Kuala Lumpur.

—It meant you were a warrior of the highest rank, Collins continued. —A man of great valor.

Spencer grew bloated with disgust. —Goddamned barbarous, if you ask me, he had said.

—Hello, Dan, he said now, shaking Collins's hand. —They asked me to come out to the office to see whether you were here.

—They?

—Feeney, I mean.

Collins grimaced.

—Eddie Gould's here, too, Spencer said.

—How is he?

There was a broad expressionlessness in Spencer's face, a look he took on when he was embarrassed. His lips were pursed.

—He's upset, Spencer said.

—How was it, bringing him out?

Spencer sat down in a chair next to Collins. He brought his fingers together over his stomach. —The bastard didn't want to come.

—What did the Ibans do?

—We didn't consider them much.

Collins played a moment with his tie. It too was moldy, in an amoeba-like paisley pattern. —When I went up there to see him, he said, —they were adamant that Eddie stay.

—Yes, that was the same for us. Spencer sat forward, placing his hands on his knees. —But there was no question about it, whether to get him out of there. I mean, I didn't even hesitate.

Spencer's eyes seemed to square behind his glasses.

—Not once, he continued. —Those Ibans may like Ed, respect him and all that.

—Love him.

—That, too. But I'll be damned if I'm going to leave him up there just because he's smitten with them.

—What about his wife?

—The girl? That was his wife?

—Yes.

Spencer rubbed his forehead with the fingers of one hand. —Jesus, that makes it even worse. There may even be a family dependents issue here. He moved toward the doorway. —Insurance.

—Insurance!

—I mean, who's liable if she has a ... you know, a baby or something?

—Liable!

Spencer opened the door, then looked back at Collins, who remained open-mouthed in his cold chair.

—You'd better come with me, Dan. We don't want to keep Feeney waiting.

Cursing under his breath, Collins stood and followed along. The two men walked together to a conference room at the far end of the hall. There were only two others in the room. They appeared to have been arguing. Eddie Gould slouched deflated in a chair at the head of the table, looking as though he had been draped over the chair to cure in the sun.

Joseph Feeney was in his late thirties, a career officer from Massachusetts, a man already thought of as a possible Secretary of State in some future administration. He was, Collins had been told, a go-getter from Harvard. Collins had met him just once before, at a reception held at the Raffles Hotel in Singapore three years previously. Along with some other State Department officials, Collins was to receive a commendation from the President of Singapore, Lee Quan Yew, for the work he had been doing in Sarawak. Right away, Collins had noticed how Feeney greeted all the Singapore government officials the same, with a quick handshake and a satisfied, forceful recitation of his name.

—Joe Feeney. Nice to see you.

The event had been held beneath a tent pavilion on the inside grounds of the hotel. It was the last such meeting before Singapore left Malaysia and became a separate nation of its own. Collins, in a coat and tie, stood quietly, sweat dribbling down his back. The heat had a palpable, glove-like feel, and Collins felt gripped by it. Even the flora appeared to suffer in the afternoon. The pearl-white blooms of the orchids hanging from vases at the entry to the Long Bar drooped like bloated rags.

The Prime Minister had been asked to present commendations to three of the American officers. Collins was cited for meritorious work on behalf of the American government for the people of Sarawak, and he was delighted to receive the recognition. His name had been mentioned around government circles quite a bit lately because of his ability to negotiate within all the different cultures he encountered. He had discovered his ability for learning languages and had moved up quickly from project to project because of it. An award like this was something that would no doubt help his career a good deal.

After the awards, Feeney delivered a speech about the privilege all Americans were so pleased to honor, to be able to help those greatly less fortunate. Lee Quan Yew maintained the air of abrupt fortitude that was present in all the photos Collins had seen of him. He did not wince at Feeney's remarks about the disenfranchised of this world, even when Feeney offered the view that his Boston stomach would probably never recover from so much curry.

Collins did wince. Standing at the edge of the pavilion, his commendation growing soggy between his fingers, he spent most of the speech gazing up at the open windows of the hotel

rooms that looked out on the grounds. All the rooms had ceiling fans, and their uniform twirl lulled Collins even more than the speech. The windows were sheltered from the sun by small awnings. Eyelids in a drowse, he thought. From his vantage point, he also saw the mosquito nets in each room, gathered up and knotted above the beds for the day, each one suspended from the ceiling on a single twine, like clouds of bunched fog.

Feeney sat now at the far end of the table from Eddie. His tie was loosened, his face blockish and youthfully craggy, with tight eyes, quite blue. Though his hair was mussed—as though he had pushed his hand through it with annoyance several times—it maintained the look Arthur Edison had complained about, of Kennedyesque, naval trim.

—Hello, Dan, he said as Collins entered the room. He stood and extended his hand. —Nice to see you.

Feeney motioned toward some chairs, and Collins sat down next to Spencer.

Right away, Collins saw that Eddie was extremely unhappy. His face was gray-yellow. Indeed he looked malnourished, his arms so thin that they seemed to come from the sleeves of his T-shirt like stems.

—Hello, Eddie, Collins said.

Eddie's glasses were still taped, the lenses quite scratched. He lifted a hand and waved at Collins. Embedded dirt made his hands look as if they had been etched with printer's ink.

—Everybody okay up there? Collins asked.

—Yeah, I guess so. Eddie sank back into the chair.

—So Eddie and I have talked about this situation, Dan, Feeney said, —and we've come to an agreement which I think will work out well for him and the Agency.

Collins glanced at Eddie, who looked down at the tabletop.

—Naturally he'll be coming back to the States with us, and ...

—Why? Collins interrupted.

Feeney, caught in mid-sentence, joined his hands. His fingers were white. So were his lips. —What do you mean, 'why?'

—Eddie's doing a fine job up there at Bintang. I could see that right away when I was there.

Eddie remained passive. But his shoulders lifted. He sat up.

—That's why you didn't say anything to us about it? Feeney replied. —Because you thought that?

—Right, Collins said.

—Sounds like you're taking the high ground, there, Dan.

—I'm just telling you the truth.

—It isn't that you were being incompetent? Feeney asked.

—No!

—Or that, for some reason, you were afraid to tell us what Eddie here had done? Feeney continued. —Maybe you were covering it up, hoping it'd go away?

—Listen ...

Feeney sat forward, and his face began to grow pink. —Forgetting *National Geographic*, for Christs's sake ...

—Listen, Eddie's the kind of guy you want in a situation like that, Collins said.

—We don't think so.

—Those people are devoted to him. He's brought them new kinds of food. They've diversified, damn it. They're healthier people.

—Listen, we ... Feeney grumbled.

—What the hell else do you want?

Tully Spencer leaned forward, his face beginning to redden as well. —Dan. Hear Joe out. He's got a point to make.

Collins sat back in his chair. His attempt to calm himself made little headway. He wanted to keep talking, but the words crowded one another inside him.

—I'll get right to the point, Feeney said. —I don't care if this guy's up there building a new Brasilia for those people, Collins. When you're with the State Department, there's a line you don't cross. And better nutrition or not ... Feeney leveled an index finger down the table at Eddie, staring at him as he spoke. —More chickens, greener beans, I don't care what it is he's doing ... He turned toward Collins. The finger remained, like a twig hanging in the air. —This guy here crossed that line.

—You haven't been up there, Collins interrupted.

—I don't need to go up there.

—You haven't seen what we're doing, Eddie suddenly interjected.

Feeney placed both hands on the table. —Listen, Eddie, you broke a lot of rules.

—But ...

—You knew what you were getting into when you went up there. You were told. In Washington. You knew you weren't supposed to get involved like that. So you're done up there. You're out!

—Joe, this is ridiculous, Collins said. The words invaded his throat. He barely knew Feeney, and was embarrassed by his use of the Undersecretary's first name. But he saw that Feeney was trying to use his office to establish some kind of moral superiority, as though what he had to say was the only truth. And Collins saw him as just a bureaucrat, doing it all by the book, when there was a far more subtle explanation to be made for Eddie's activities at Bintang.

—What gives you the right to make such a decision? Collins demanded. —You don't know what's going on out here. You don't know how good Eddie is!

Feeney turned toward Collins. His eyes grew smaller. They got more intensely blue, and he frowned.

—I don't know how good he is? Feeney asked.

—That's right.

Feeney lifted his hand into the air once more. This time, the accusing index finger was aimed at Collins himself.

—Okay, Collins. Then you're out, too, he said.

—Joe! Spencer shook his head. —Wait a minute. Dan's the best guy we've got out here.

—Not anymore, Feeney said. —You're on your way to Washington, Collins. The plane leaves here tomorrow morning. I'll be on it. And so will Eddie. The two of you can sit together if you like.

—But what about my wife? Eddie panicked.

—You'll get to write to her, Feeney said.

—Write to her! Eddie looked across the table at Collins, his eyes large and damp, as though a ruinous secret had been exposed. —She can't read!

That afternoon, Collins arrived back in Simanngang and drove his Land Rover to his house in Kampong Ayer. It was an old wooden building surrounded by coconut palms, a quarter mile from the Chinese bazaar. He walked up the stairs and entered the living room, dropping his shoulder bag to the floor. He removed the new straw hat he had bought in Kuching and flung it to the floor as well. He sat down on a batik pillow against the wall, beneath a large mounted shadow-puppet. The puppet's head was thrust back, so that the mouth and eyes faced the ceiling in a skeletal laugh. Collins rested his elbows on his knees. He had no idea how he would gather all his belongings together on so little notice.

Irresolute, mumbling, he stood and walked to his bedroom. His clothes hung on hangers from a wooden pole extended horizontally across a corner of the room. He had not worn most of them for years. Sportcoats, ties, dress shirts—all of them leftovers from his apartment in San Francisco. He recalled once more his drawing board at AB Engineering Systems, a bland plane on which he had carefully arranged his T-squares and triangles. Everything on the table had been white or clear, and he remembered how he had often thought of himself, then, as being made up of the same colors.

His revery was interrupted by the voice of Mrs. Zainal next door, a widow who did Collins's washing. Collins looked out the window. Mrs. Zainal yelled at her grandson Achmed to bring the durian fruit he was selling in from the sun, that it would get overripe otherwise. —Nobody'll buy it, she said. She was a withered, skinny woman, brightly dressed in a red and green batik sarong. —It smells awful already. Her high voice rose up like a seabird's.

Achmed stepped out from beneath the palm tree where he had been sitting. He was six years old, and he wore a pair of underpants. He began rolling one of the durian, the size of a small bowling ball, toward the shade. Collins looked beyond the boy at the neighboring houses. Cooking smoke hung like swatches of blue gauze through the trees. The trunks of palms curved upward, slim lines bursting into fronds, as though into frivolous laughter.

He fingered the dress shirt hanging before him. His heart seemed to grow in his chest, painfully so, to hurt with the pressure that contained it. He looked out once more into his living-room. There was a pair of canvas chairs, several photos on one wall, a bookshelf, a table.

Nothing.

He pushed two pairs of shorts into his shoulder bag with two extra shirts, making sure he had his passport and other papers, his sunglasses, a penlight, and his wallet. He put on the straw hat and slammed the door of his house as he left.

Passing Achmed on the path, he squatted down before the boy.

—How much for one of those, Achmed? he asked in Malay.

—One *ringgit* each, Tuan, the boy said. He appeared surprised, knowing, as did all the neighbors, that the American could not stomach the sickly alcoholic stench of the fruit so loved by all the Malays. Collins reached into his pocket and produced a single bill.

—Achmed! Mrs. Zainal shouted. Collins and the boy looked about. The old woman stood on her porch, a cloth dripping water in her hands. —That's for the Tuan?

—Yes, Grandmother. The boy's voice sounded threatened, as though he were being scolded.

—For you, Tuan, it's free. Mrs. Zainal's face broke into a smile. She had no teeth.

—Here. Take the money anyway, Achmed. Collins slipped it into the boy's hand, then placed a finger against his own lips, implying the secrecy of the gift he was giving Achmed. Tipping his hat to Mrs. Zainal, he took up the durian. He walked to the road, checked to make sure his Land Rover was securely locked, and headed into town.

It was a few minutes' walk through the Simanggang bazaar to the Chartered Bank of England. Collins hurried along, trying to get down the dirt street of the market without being hailed by the shopkeepers, most of whom he knew. Simanggang was the capital of the Second Division and, as such, a major center of commerce. There was even an Iban market there every Saturday. It was not much competition to the Chinese bazaar, since it occupied a vacant lot between two wooden shop buildings, and was made up of three or four woven blankets spread out on the ground, each one looked after by an Iban woman. There was little for sale. The women sat beneath a ragged cloth tent held up on bamboo sticks. Collins scurried by, intent on the far end of the street.

—Tuan!

He continued walking.

—Beans, Tuan!

Collins checked his shoulder bag, attempting a look of distracted bustle.

—Your favorite!

The woman's voice was so shrill, especially as it broke into a clatter of talk, that Collins could proceed no farther. He turned and waved. He knew her well.

Lena sat by her blanket, holding a half dozen green beans in a soiled hand. Her mouth contained three brown teeth. The black cloth she had wrapped about her head had a woven black and red border; it too was very dirty, yet it was carefully tied, so her gray hair would not come loose. She was the wife of Big Penan, a farmer from Rumah Utan, which was on the main road three miles from Simanngang. Collins made a point of stopping to buy a few things from the Iban women whenever he was in the market on a Saturday. Lena liked him, her feelings for him evident in her abrasive merriment.

—In a hurry, Tuan? she said as, finally, Collins turned to acknowledge her. —You won't try my beans?

Collins hunkered down before her blanket. —Of course I will, he said in Iban. He lay the durian on the blanket and reached into his bag for money. —In fact I thought you might like to have that. He nodded toward the fruit.

—Oh. Big Penan loves the durian, Lena said. She rolled the fruit toward her and secured it in the cloth bag at her side. —Even though the Malays charge too much for it.

She spoke with the rough accent of the upriver Third Division Ibans, who were considered crass but humorous by those down here in Simanggang. Above the Belaga rapids, on the Rajang

River, there had been no English missionaries and few travelers of any kind. As far as the downriver Ibans were concerned, the people who came from that deep in the mountains were a far-away mystery. There, the forest enveloped the people in watery heat. The trees grew so close and huge that the people resorted to all their old-time magic and beliefs to protect themselves from the jungle's secret terrors. Such notions had been set aside in the downriver regions by the kindly Anglican missionaries who had lived here during the past hundred years or so.

Collins knew little about upper Rajang, but he did know that the Ibans in Simanggang seemed to envy those from Belaga and farther up. The feathered fetishes, flying warrior-spirits, ghost-women, god-birds, warlocks, and wraiths that they still so readily believed in there carried more actual authority than the gray-beard Englishman that the white men had brought along with them as their god, so bland and distant.

Lena's accent was old-fashioned, and the other women kidded her for it. She had been brought to Simanggang by Big Penan, who had gone on his *bejelai* as a youth, up the Rajang. Collins had been told that Lena had been quite beautiful as a girl. Now, she had numerous grandchildren, and her features were thick with wrinkles and the damage brought on by working so many years in the damp, bright heat. Her earlobes were broken, having been overstretched by the brass rings she had worn in them as a girl. Collins had noticed that the graceful dignity of her walk, caused by many years of balancing the weight of the rings, still remained, though she had probably not worn them for thirty years. Her shredded earlobes waved in the air like tassels.

There was a pile of loose tobacco on Lena's blanket, some of which she took between her fingers to roll into a cigarette. Collins took a Red Chinese Zippo from his shirt pocket and lit it for her. The other women, sitting at their blankets in a line next to Lena's, listened as the two acquaintances spoke.

—You seem so much in a hurry, she said, lifting the cigarette to her lips.

—I'm going on a trip, Collins said.

—Ah. Where to?

So recently a fugitive … just for the past few minutes, actually … Collins realized to his considerable surprise that what he now was planning was directly counter to Feeney's order to report back to Kuching that evening.

—We expected better from you, Dan, a lot better, the Under-secretary had said.

The disdain in his voice had caused Collins's ire to flame with hurt intensity. He had left the office immediately, returned to His Majesty's Arms, and checked out without a word to John Bull, who waved at him from the dining hall as the screen door crashed behind him.

Collins had not even asked himself where he was going. He was shocked by the notion of even *being* a fugitive, and wondered where he had gotten it. Such people ran from hostile authorities. They were criminals and had much to hide. But in Collins's case, what he was running from had remained hidden until this moment, and Lena's question. It had been obscured by the cumulative effect of all the time he had spent learning the languages he spoke, of feeling the sweat cascade down his trunk, of nursing cuts that would not heal, and examining intricate woven cloth in faraway longhouses. It had been obscured by the simple admiration of the view over the gunnels of a longboat floating free down a glass-clear jungle river. By the green, damp shade.

Witnessing similar pleasures being taken from Eddie Gould with so little thought and regret, Collins realized how little he really owed the State Department. And it was from that … the State Department's self-assured correctness and blindness … that Collins was running. Eddie had been right. He had found love in the jungle, and his being forced by his colleagues from the woods had left a wounded emptiness.

—I'm on my way to Sibu, Collins said with sudden clarity.

—From there I'll go up the Rajang, I suppose.

—But you don't know where?

Lena passed Collins a handful of beans, which he placed in his bag. He remained in the shade of the pavilion, wiping his forehead with a sleeve.

—Will you go as far as Belaga? she asked.

—Farther.

—Into the mountains? The look on Lena's face was a rueful one. She knew Collins had traveled quite a bit in Sarawak, but there was in her look the suggestion that he may not have seen the things he would see in upper Rajang.

—It's possible, yes.

—You're looking for a wife? Lena asked.

The other women broke into laughter.

—Nice girls up there, Lena said, —who know how to cook and work. Not like these. Lena thrust a hand toward the others, who enjoyed her chiding.

—No, I just ... want to see what's up there.

—Then you should go to my longhouse, Tuan. Rumah Nadai. There is nothing there.

—Nothing! Then why go?

—I mean, nothing that you know. No white people. No Land Rovers. No Muslims, none of those. There, there is only the forest, Tuan. The rain. The rivers.

Lena nodded toward the others.

—You know Big Penan, she said. —He's a fine hunter. He knows how to use the blowgun, doesn't he? which no one here uses any more.

The women nodded agreement.

—But even Big Penan, Tuan, was amazed by what he saw up there. He says that, before he went there, he had seen such things only in his dreams. You can't just walk through the forest. You must know the way.

—Is it difficult to find?

—Rumah Nadai? No. You just go four days' travel above Belaga, on the main river. Ask, as you get farther up. The Ibans will direct you. The people there are kind. They won't ...

Lena paused and searched Collins's eyes.

—They won't take your head, Tuan.

Abruptly, all the women laughed. Collins did not think there was anything comic about his reaction. He simply stood before the women, his mouth open in search of a reply. But then he saw that the women's laughter was quite nervous.

He moved on to the Chartered Bank of England. It was a low-ceilinged shop five doors up the bazaar from the women's market, a large single room open to the street. Its walls were stained with years of mold, so that they appeared woven, a wet abstract of browns and greens. A counter ran the width of the entry. Immediately behind it was a wooden desk on which were two enormous ledger books and a half glass of hot tea. A tin ashtray was filled to overflowing with cigarette butts while a fan twirled from the ceiling, causing the top pages of the ledgers to flap up and down at the corners.

Charles Parnell Yee was the manager, a banker with whom Collins had kept his account since his arrival in Sarawak, when he had been assigned to the Second Division. Collins was considered a prestigious customer, because he was the only government officer in Simanggang whose paycheck came directly to the bank from the American Embassy in Kuala Lumpur. Parnell therefore put on an air of suave self-importance when Collins came to visit, as though he were the executor of his estate, his personal solicitor, perhaps. He was a Fu-chou Chinese from Sibu, and his English was quite good.

He sat at one of the ledgers as Collins entered the bank. There were three other employees, in *songkoks*, all of them Malays. They occupied separate, smaller desks, each with his own ledger book. They worked intently at writing out information on scraps of paper, which they handed back and forth to each other.

—Mr. Collins!

—Hello, Parnell, Collins replied. He dropped his bag to the counter and took Parnell's hand. —How are you?

—Excellent. Parnell turned to the other employees and gestured toward Collins. —You blighters remember our American friend, yes?

There was general acknowledgment of Collins's presence, but he knew that Parnell was just trying to flatter him. To Collins's knowledge, none of the Malays spoke any English at all. And of course they knew Collins well.

Parnell was fifty-five years old, a stocky man whose open-collared white shirt bulged out over his belt. He always seemed intent on appearing prosperous, and he was exceedingly friendly to Collins, once having him as guest of honor at a New Year's banquet at the cafe next door to the bank. At the end of the evening, Collins's shirt had ended up sprinkled with pork gravy and Hennessy Five-Star. Parnell had personally escorted the wobbly American back home, where he had left him stretched out in a chair for the night. Collins liked Parnell because he helped him with information about cargoboat schedules, ways of shipping supplies, particular boat drivers who were honest and those who were not.

—Someday, though, I'll be coming to take all my money out, Collins had once said.

—Yes, Parnell replied. —Sad day.

—It will be?

—Yes. Americans take their money away, you know … He adjusted his glasses, his head beginning to quiver with enjoyment of his joke. —Chartered Bank of England lose charter.

—Parnell, Collins said now, opening his bag and removing his passport. —Today's the day. He slipped the passport onto the counter. —I need my money.

Rearranging the other things in his bag, he did not notice Parnell's silence. When he looked up, he surveyed Parnell's eyes, which appeared to be made of glass.

—Is there a problem? Collins asked.

—Problem? No. No problem, Mr. Collins. We have, though …

Parnell turned and took up the ledger. Staggering briefly beneath its weight, he carried it to the counter. —We have procedures.

—What procedures?

—I must contact England.

—England!

—Yes. Permission, you know.

—But it's my money.

—Quite right. But Chartered Bank of England must protect itself.

—You have to go all the way to England?

Parnell began turning pages in the ledger. The sound of them, like slabs of rubber falling against one another, distracted Collins.

—I just send them telex, you see.

—I see.

—Well, I don't send telex. I radio-telephone first to Kuching. As Parnell spoke, his hands followed a tortured route around one another, fingers in various directions. —They radio-telephone to Kuala Lumpur, and then *they* telex.

—To London.

—Yes.

Collins leaned over the counter as Parnell turned the pages once more.

—That will take a while, Collins said.

—One week.

—A week!

Startled, Parnell looked over the tops of his glasses at Collins.

—But it's my money, Collins repeated.

—We cannot let money go so simply, Mr. Collins. Chartered Bank of England must protect.

—Against what?

—People maybe not so honest as you and me.

Collins took up his passport and thumbed through it. —But I'm the one who put it in. And it's me who's taking it out.

Parnell found the page for which he was searching and ran an index finger down the numbers and names along the left margin.

—Ah, he said. —You have balance of three hundred seventy thousand *ringgit*. That is seventy-four thousand dollars U.S.

Collins's certainty wavered. —Seventy-four thousand?

—You want all?

Since there was almost no need for funds of any kind out here, Collins simply had not kept track of his pay over the years. This was an enormous sum of money.

—I guess I do, he said.

Parnell shook his head. —Mr. Collins, I cannot. He looked down at the ledger once more, mortified. —I just cannot. Not without permission of London.

Collins found that, really, he had no argument with Parnell. He was just tied up in regulations—regulations that had been enacted over centuries maybe—and he simply would not break them. Besides, Collins asked himself, what'll you do at Rumah Nadai with such a fortune? The rules he was running from were less hide-bound than those of the Chartered Bank of England, but equally strict and greatly more powerful. The only cure for such bureaucracy was escape.

—Can you give me anything? Collins asked.

Parnell looked over his shoulder. The clerks had turned back to their tasks and now paid little attention to the conversation.

—I can maybe make you a loan, against next time you come to visit us, he said. —Out of ordinary, of course.

—I'm good for it, Parnell. You know that.

—Yes, yes. But are you coming back?

—I don't know. Why?

Parnell looked down at the counter. —Usually, somebody wants to take out seventy-four thousand dollars U.S., he is preparing himself to leave.

—How much can you lend me?

Parnell looked about the room, then went to his desk to open one of its drawers. He took out a metal cashbox, which he opened. —Two hundred *ringgit,* he sighed after a moment. He raised his shoulders in a shrug. —And I must get Kuching's permission, Parnell continued. His voice grew tight and miserable.

—Radio-telephone, Collins said.

—Yes, Mr. Collins, Parnell bowed. —Yes.

They hurried into the street and walked toward the District Officer's office. By now, the sun was lowering. Ascending the stairs to the D.O.'s, the two men remained silent, though Collins sensed that Parnell feared he was in some sort of trouble for being so uncooperative with the American. Sweat had soaked the back of Parnell's shirt. His hair was mussed.

Placing a hand on his shoulder, Collins attempted to calm him. —I appreciate this, he said. But even this had an edgy tone to it, and Parnell did not reply.

After ten minutes' wait, Parnell got through to Kuching. There was an argumentative conversation, in which the banker had to speak with several people in a couple of languages. Finally he gave Collins a thumbs-up and ended the phone call with a number of grateful pleasantries.

—They'll let us do it, even without the proper ... what is it, paper play?

—Paper work.

—That's right. Parnell shook his head. —Out of ordinary, you know.

They returned to the bank. Parnell took several forms from his desk drawers, and he and Collins filled them out in triplicate. Then Parnell gave some of the forms to one clerk and the rest to another. The two men proofread them, did the sums on their abacuses, stamped the forms, tore them into individual parts, and exchanged them with each other for further notation. All the pieces were filed and, as Collins paced the floor, the original copy of each was given back to Parnell. The banker took out the cashbox once more and counted out one hundred ninety-eight *ringgit.*

—Sorry, he said, as he handed the money to Collins with a receipt and his passport. —There's a fee.

Collins surveyed the bills. The paltry sum deflated him. —Forget it, he said. Stuffing the money into his wallet, he slung his bag over his shoulder and extended his hand to Parnell. —I know how difficult it is to bend the rules, Collins muttered.

—Jolly well impossible, Parnell replied. Collins turned and headed into the street.

—But what about the rest of your money? Parnell called.

Collins looked back. Parnell stood behind the counter, his hands outspread on the wood. The clerks looked out as well, though Collins could see only their heads above the level of the counter, like cheery jars.

—I'll be back, Collins replied.

—When?

Not answering, Collins turned up the street toward the bus station.

73

The late afternoon sun hung over the coconut trees at the end of the bazaar. The Iban women were folding their blankets, while Lena herself took down the cloth pavilion and began rolling it up. Heading for the station, Collins saw that he still had some time before he had to leave. He walked toward the women who, noting his approach, stopped their work.

—I'll be going in five minutes, Collins said as he squatted before Lena's blanket. She sat down at his side, adjusting the rag on her head. She had packed her leftover goods in a black cloth, and her money was secured in a belt around her waist.

Collins removed his straw hat. So new, it retained a prim freshness that, compared with his stubbled hands, was even elegant. The cuts he had got on his fingers—so difficult to heal in the jungle dampness—now seemed themselves decayed. The skin appeared ruined after so many years' working on machinery, digging holes, lugging equipment up mud riverbanks from longboats. But the hat was fresh. It had youth and simple lines, as perhaps Collins had had when he first arrived in Sarawak.

But after a moment, the comparison seemed pointless and trite. He was just feeling sorry for himself. His usual hope that he was a conscientious man of good humor now appeared so impertinent as to have no importance at all. He had become a fool.

But he could not figure out what sort of fool. Was he going native, like Eddie? Was he one of those? Betrayed by whatever family or bureaucracy, they thumbed their nose at where they had come from. They became instantly rustic, they refused visitors, and they inveighed, even angrily, against whatever it was that had driven them so far into the jungle, the sierra, the bush, or the outback … wherever it was they had decided to make their complaining abode. Was he one of those?

—I have a cousin at Rumah Nadai, Lena said. —Ibu's her name. She's the Chinese man's wife.

—Chinese? Up there?

—Yes. He's the only one. He thinks he's Iban.

Collins placed the hat on his head. —I'll look for her, he said. —Do you have any other advice for me?

—Just, at night, watch out for the darkness.

Lena made this remark without reflection, busying herself with her preparations to leave. It was offhand, a throwaway. Yet, it contained a threat. Collins awaited more, something specific about the colors in the jungle after sundown maybe, about the kind of rain there was or the odor of the trails in the dark early mornings.

Up the street, the engines of two buses turned over into a roar. Collins stood and placed the hat on his head. Several latecomers ran toward the bus station.

—Take someone with you when you go out, that's all, Lena said. —The jungle there is difficult, Tuan. Especially at night.

Collins nodded and turned away. He headed for the buses. One of them, marked with a sign over the windshield that read

KUCHING, had begun pulling out. The driver halted, holding a hand up toward Collins, who waved him away. Instead he approached the second bus, marked SARIKEI, which would take him in the opposite direction. Greeting the driver, he hurried up the three steps and into a seat. He would spend the night in Sarikei and catch a taxiboat the next morning before dawn for Sibu, up the Rajang River.

The following daybreak, there were many cargo boats taking on freight at the Sibu docks. One of them rode low in the water and already had several passengers. It was the only one of the boats at the wharf to have its name printed in English as well as Chinese. But the words were almost indistinguishable, erased by heavy weather and age, so that *New Happiness* was now merely a ghostly suggestion.

A half hour later, the *New Happiness* pulled away from the Sibu wharf and turned upriver. Collins leaned on the railing of the upper deck, looking out at the waterfront buildings. They were no different from those Collins had seen elsewhere hundreds of times ... corrugated iron sheds dotted with rust on wooden pilings. But there was music coming from one of the warehouses, a large storage building that sagged on its pilings. It was not the kind of music Collins would have expected, having none of the dreaminess prevalent in

5

Malay lovesongs, their effortless duet voices floating about, sensuous and interwoven. Nor was there the abrupt jangle of popular Chinese music. Instead, this was choral and Western-minded. It was the Beach Boys in church ... "Good, good, good, good vibrations."

Though it was only seven-thirty in the morning, the air on the river was already wet and hot. It could not be moved. Collins waited for the breeze he knew would come as the boat headed upriver, but the palms on either bank remained still. So did the plume of smoke left by the *New Happiness,* an undefined, gray bag that hung a few feet above the surface behind the retreating cargo boat. The water parted to allow the boat's passage ... but reluctantly, as though it were made of oil. The waves surged toward the banks in a curving V but did little to disrupt the surface itself, which remained flat and embedded with water lilies, like a decorated griddle.

Collins descended some wooden stairs to the lower deck, where much of the foodstuff cargo was piled up fore and aft —numerous sacks of rice, crates filled with tinned goods, and rope-sacks bulging with vegetables. The deck was open to the river on both sides, and about twenty Ibans sat on the large hatch that covered the cargo hold. Most had fallen asleep as soon as the boat left the wharf, and now lay propped up on rice sacks. There were several fighting cocks in rope cages. Three large river fish hung on a line suspended from a nail, and drops of their blood sullied the hatch cover below them. Nearby, a full-grown pig was trussed up in lengths of thick jute that, wrapped all around him, made a kind of straitjacket. The pig complained, but its squeals had little effect on the Iban man sleeping next to it. The only Malay passenger was seated on the far side of the hatch cover, facing away from the pig and muttering about it. The blasphemy of transporting such an animal on the same boat as a Muslim, he said to Collins, was an insult to the faithful. The Ibans were to be damned for it. So were the Chinese.

—Don't you think so, Tuan? he asked. He was a young man, clear-eyed and official-looking, possibly a government officer. He wore a white shirt.

Collins shrugged.

He sat down on the hatch to look out at the river. Flowing, as it does, from the mountains, and being a major conduit of water to the coast from a half dozen tributaries, the Rajang is a surging river, quite deep, that moves with such force that traffic going upriver must actually struggle against it. Big cargo boats like the *New Happiness* attacked the flow with engines and noise. The Iban and Malay fishermen, whose longboats were powered mostly by paddle, huddled close to the banks, where the flow was much milder.

Over the mountains ahead, gray clouds had begun gathering, and now, finally, the wind started blowing, stirring the coconut palms on the banks. The clouds had appeared quickly and darkened as they lowered to the mountains themselves. Within minutes, the palms were leaning with the wind, falling back against it, and leaning once more. White chop appeared on the river surface, and soon thereafter the *New Happiness* steamed into a squall making its way down from the mountains. The sky darkened far ahead to resemble a canopy of stone.

In the mountains themselves, there was little differentiation beween the earth and the clouds. Both were obscured by the rain, so that the dank mist surrendered itself to the canyons and embraced the worn-looking peaks. Suddenly, the storm broke into a melee, sending water crashing into the ironwood trees, into the recesses of the river where fishermen had retreated to wait it out, and all over the *New Happiness*. Water flailed from the surfaces of the cargo boat like wind-strewn oil. No matter what protection Collins sought, he was soaked with rain as the boat pushed up the current toward the mountains.

After several hours more, the boat entered a wide part of the Rajang and turned toward Kanowit, a town on the southern bank, at the mouth of the tributary Kanowit River. There seemed to be little difference between the river and the shore. When the gangplank was finally lowered to the wharf, Collins hurried down it. He headed for a cafe in the bazaar, throwing his arm up to keep the rain from his face.

Several Chinese workers sat at tables inside the cafe, drinking tea. Though they were not surprised to see a European in the town—Kanowit was a district office and had therefore been governed by numerous Englishmen—Collins's appearance provoked some interest, especially when he began asking in Iban for transport up the river. He wanted to go to Belaga, he said, and then to continue farther up, into the mountains.

—Belaga, yes, one of the Chinese said. Indeed he was a boatman, and was leaving within the hour. —But we won't take you past Belaga, Tuan. From there, you have to find an Iban to take you.

—Why?

The boatman sat on a wooden chair, his feet up on the seat. His toes were stained with engine oil. A piece of cotton was wrapped about his head. Outside, the monsoon spilled from the sky.

—The upriver Ibans, they don't like us, the boatman said.

He looked about the shop, seeking agreement. The roar of the water against the tin roof seemed to emphasize the cafe's airlessness.

—They don't like boatmen? Collins asked.

—No. They don't like Chinese! The boatman made a fist and brought it toward his neck, as though it were holding a knife. He made a sawing motion next to his throat, then pretended to yank his head into the air. —Some Chinese used to go up there, the man continued. —But no more.

The others agreed, nodding at each other and adding long observations in the Cantonese dialect. Collins understood none of them.

—You're sure you want to go, John? the boat driver asked. The name "John" was an insult—like "bub" or "gringo"—used only for Englishmen. The others in the cafe waited in silence, and Collins sensed that, in fact, they might be worried about him.

—Yes, Collins replied. He reached for his bag. —How much?

Hours later, the boat on which Collins was a passenger approached the base of the Belaga rapids. Water came down the river in a seeming cloud of white, emerging from a deep roar. The boats gathered a hundred yards below the rapids, waiting for room at the small docks on the riverbank, where passengers were disembarking.

—You get out here, the boatman shouted. Collins could barely hear him over the sound of the river. —We take the boat up. You walk.

Collins grabbed his gear and stepped out onto the bank. A path paralleling the river led into the forest, and Collins followed passengers from other boats—Ibans, for the most part, traveling to Belaga to sell vegetables to the Chinese in the bazaar—as they began the mile-long trek to the top of the rapids.

Collins himself had gone upriver through systems of rapids many times. But he had never seen such gigantic force as the Rajang had. The water blurred where it flew over the larger boulders. It reared up in jagged plumes, then fell to the surface of the river, to be swept past the next boulders into huge, swirling blowholes.

The boats started out well below the rapids, heading straight for the main channel leading up through several granite boulders. Empty of passengers, their outboard engines seemed too large for the boats, until the force of the water coming down showed how quickly they could be paralyzed in the middle of a narrow strait. At times, though the engines were opened to full throttle, the boats shuddered and crept backwards. A few men stood on high rocks between which the boats would navigate, to act as guides for the crewmen. The men on the boulders shouted, urging the engines on, horrified by the possibility of their failing.

Collins imagined one of the boats, suddenly without power, shredding as it capsized over a jagged escarpment. Pointing at hidden shoals and whirlpools, the guides panicked when a boat came too close. When their voices rose above the noise of the river, they did so incoherently, in rapid pecks of sound. The men waved their hands. They screamed. Looking down through the rain from the path, Collins often could not see what a specific danger was, so that the men seemed to be pointing into violent invisibility.

At the top of the rapids, the boats pulled once more to the bank and took on their passengers. From there they made their way through a much thicker forest, through which the gray light barely glimmered. This forest was not benign like the one downriver, and Collins knew that this was because it had never been cut down. The jungle around the town of Simanggang was like scrub compared with this. But the land there had been cultivated for centuries, and the jungle seemed friendly to the farmland. Up here, Collins had entered the beginnings of the rain forest. The longhouses were fewer and sheltered in the darkness of the jungle.

As he continued up the river, Collins wondered how such a forest could be negotiated at all. Pathways seemed cut off even at the moment they entered the jungle. Children played on the riverbanks, as they did everywhere he had been in Sarawak. Women washed their clothes. But up and down this part of the river, the people seemed to cling to the line of sand that formed the bank and the several square yards of cleared land where they had constructed their longhouses, as though going into the forest itself were not possible.

From a distance, the buildings of the Belaga bazaar appeared beaten down by the dusk storm. The town oozed, hunkering on the bank, a junkyard of wood and tin. The wharves were just a collection of planks nailed to sodden beams, tied to the shore with jute. Stepping out of the boat, Collins held his pack in his arms. Looking downriver, he could not really see where the river entered the forest. It darkened as it descended and simply disappeared.

He ascended a log on the mud bank and walked into the bazaar. A cafe was lit by gas lanterns. The other shops were already closed, and the wooden sidewalks on stilts were like sieves, straining the rainwater that poured through them to the mud below. Collins went up some steps and entered the cafe.

There were three tables. The owner, a Chinese sitting at a cash drawer at the rear of the cafe, looked up from his newspaper. He wore steel-rimmed glasses. He lay the paper down and glanced at the other patrons, all three of whom sat at a single table.

They were Ibans. But they were unlike any Collins had ever seen. In loincloths, they squatted on the chairs rather than sitting on them, their feet tucked up beneath their haunches. They smoked homemade cigarettes, and their *parangs* hung in sheaths from their waists. One of the men groomed a fighting cock that sat on his lap. Another leaned against a blowpipe, as though it were a staff. To Collins, they made up a tableau of savagery, their silent perusal of him actually frightening. But he knew these men were not savages. What made them seem so was his memory of everything he had read in the San Francisco library about the Serengeti Plain, the Masai, Bengal tigers, bloodthirsty Malay pirates. In short, all those adventure books filled with buccaneers, great white hunters, and bush pilots.

The Ibans did not speak. Tattooed and golden-skinned in the gray roar of the storm, they seemed unimpressed with Collins, amused maybe, and threatening. But when Collins ordered a Coca Cola from the proprietor and mentioned in Iban the ferocity of the rain, they looked at each other with silent and suddenly warming surprise.

—Tuan. The man with the blowpipe leaned forward and dropped his cigarette to the floor. He stamped it out with his foot, and beckoned toward Collins once more. —Tuan.

Collins looked about, raising the soft drink to his lips.

—I'm Bawang, the Iban said. —Are you going up the river? You want to go into the forest?

For a moment, Collins did not speak. Bawang's two companions simply stared at him, as though Collins were an exhibit at a museum. But he felt he must be a poor exhibit, badly put together maybe and, as a result, boring. Neither of the men really reacted to him. Their eyes were luminous, but blank. After a moment, Collins realized that the men were astonished by him. Their leaden insistence on watching him was the result of anxiety. On his own, with his muddy shoulder bag and bedraggled hat, Collins was a vision.

—Yes, that's where I'm going, Collins replied. —But I don't know the way.

—Which house?

—Nadai.

Bawang wrapped both hands around his blowpipe and rested his cheek against it. He wore a necklace made of a few strands of leather and some crude brass rings.

—It's a long way, he said.

—Can you take me? I'll pay you.

—Pay? To take a tuan to Nadai? Bawang looked about the room and broke into a smile. His teeth were black. —Tuan. That's my house. I'm the headman there. It will be an honor.

Collins and Bawang followed the river on foot for four days, stopping in longhouses along the way. Collins's stamina flagged, owing to the rugged terrain and the celebratory parties thrown for him at each of the houses. He had grown used to this when working with the Ibans himself. When a Tuan arrived, they could not help honoring the moment. At first, Collins had resisted these events, until he realized it was an insult to the Ibans to do so. His negotiations with the headman over some project the government wanted to do would be put aside in favor of *tuak*, *gamelan* music, and dance. After some years, Collins had mastered the ability to explain himself and the government's wishes while oawash in song and laughter.

When they arrived at a large house, at a widening in the river called Long Anak, Bawang told Collins that they had only about four hours' walk farther through the forest to get to Nadai. It was ten in the morning, and Collins wanted to continue on so that they could arrive well before sundown. But the headman at Long Anak, whose name was Jugeh, insisted that there be a gathering honoring Collins's presence in the forest. Bawang delivered a speech, apologizing for the fact that the tuan did not wish for a party, that he was on an important government mission, that in essence he could not dally. But Jugeh insisted that they at least have lunch, and Collins and Bawang barely got away three hours later, after each had had many glasses of *tuak*.

Several hours later Collins and Bawang stopped as they heard voices up ahead. They were deep in the forest. The constant rain dripped unevenly through the trees. A longboat was moored to the riverbank, thirty yards down from the end of a longhouse. A plank decking had been added to the boat, as well as a low, shed-like structure toward the rear. There seemed to be no one on the boat just now, though Collins heard more talk coming from the longhouse itself. Bawang tapped his shoulder and gestured toward the building.

—Welcome, Tuan, he said. He adjusted the sack he had strapped to his back. —Welcome to Rumah Nadai. They continued down the path to the riverbank.

Collins leaned over to look inside the boat. The cabin was a squat shack made of dried-out palm fronds laid across a wooden frame. There was no one inside, and Collins was surprised to see what looked like shelving along one gunnel, filled with colorfully labeled tins. There was a small table at the far end, on which rested an abacus in a wooden box. A Chinese newspaper was opened up on the table, next to a lit cigarette in a metal ashtray. Water continued falling from the trees. Each drop made a distinct, startling sound, like a stick being broken.

—Well-koam. The voice startled Collins, especially its formal, mispronounced English. The two syllables sounded like closing doors.

A Chinese man, dressed in khaki shorts held up with a piece of jute, and a pair of flip-flops, descended the bank from the longhouse. He was very dark and so thin that his stringy musculature appeared to be permanently tight, like stretched rope. His legs were bowed, and, as he walked, the flip-flops slapped the bottoms of his feet. He was accompanied by an Iban woman who had wrapped a cloth around her shoulders for protection against the rain. Her hair was iron-gray and she had a basket cradled in one arm that contained slices of fresh pork. The man carried a plastic bottle on one shoulder, filled with gasoline. A rooster was cradled beneath his free arm, clucking as its owner approached Collins.

—Where did you find this one? the Chinese, in Iban, asked Bawang. He nodded toward Collins.

—In Belaga.

—The government sent him?

—No. He was by himself.

—Will you take him a moment, Tuan? the man said, handing the rooster to the American. Collins noted that he spoke Iban with barely an accent. He took the rooster in his hands, worried that the bird would peck at him. Its wattle jiggled back and forth with each jerk of its head.

—I trade cigarettes with one of the Ibans here for the gasoline, see, the man said. He placed one foot onto the bow of the boat and dropped the bottle to the deck. He brushed off his hands, looking back at Collins. His front teeth were edged with gold.

—He has many boats, while I have ...

The Chinese looked down at the splintered deck.

—I have just this.

His hand moved to the back of his neck.

—It needs caulk, he concluded, his shoulders sagging.

—What's your name? Collins asked.

—Chiang, the man said. He wiped his hands on his shorts. He

beckoned for the rooster. Securing the bird with a string just beneath the edge of the frond roof, Chiang reached into his pocket and pulled out some grains of cooked rice, which he sprinkled on the deck.

—And your wife, Collins said. He smiled at the woman, who looked away shyly. —She's ...

—Yes, from this longhouse, Chiang said.

—She's my sister! Bawang said.

—She is? And the boat?

—My shop. Chiang stepped up onto the bow and motioned toward Collins. —Come in, he said. —It's raining too hard to stay out here.

There was hardly enough room for the four people. Collins, Bawang, and the woman sat down on squared-off blocks of wood that served as chairs. Chiang excused himself, scuttling past them toward the table, next to which was a similar piece of wood, to which he lowered himself. He took up his cigarette and placed it between his lips. Squinting, he reached into a cubbyhole next to the table and brought out a packet of Chinese cigarettes, which he offered to Collins.

—You are English, Tuan, he asserted.

—No. American.

—American! Chiang took the cigarette from his lips. A soft puff of smoke came from his mouth and swirled about before him. —I never saw an American before.

The following silence was sharpened by the steady rain tippling on the roof above.

—There aren't many of us here, Collins replied. —I mean in Borneo.

—That is certainly so, Chiang said. He watched as Collins lit the cigarette. —Here at Rumah Nadai, for instance, there are none.

Collins snapped the lighter shut and looked out past the rooster at the longhouse up the bank. —So this is Lena's house.

—You know her, Tuan? the woman suddenly interjected.

—My cousin?

—You're Ibu?

—That's right. And it's been so long since Lena left. She's all right? Her husband is well?

Ibu's obvious pleasure brought a grin to her face, and Collins noted the resemblance she had to Lena, how their smiles made them look so much younger.

—They're still in Simanggang. She told me about this place.

Chiang placed the cigarette in the ashtray and reached across the table to one of the shelves. There was a small box of Chinese candies, which he handed to Collins. The American reached into his pocket for some money, but Chiang waved it away.

—Lena told me about you, too, Collins said. —But it's almost as strange to see a Chinese this far up the river as it is an American.

He passed the candies to Bawang.

—I know. But the people here are very kind.

—How long have you been here?

—Thirty years. I came here looking for a wife. The people here aren't like Ibans elsewhere.

—How so?

—They don't treat the Chinese with contempt, Chiang said. There was a downturn in his voice, a note of reflective disappointment.

—But do many Chinese come here?

—No. I think they're too afraid to.

—Then do the Ibans treat you with kindness because you're the only one they've ever seen?

Chiang looked out at the longhouse, then at Bawang. The labels of the tins arrayed along the shelves showed lychee fruit, fish, corn, and green beans. There were a half dozen pairs of new flip-flops hanging from a string, and several packets of cigarettes in a carton. Five bottles of Coca Cola were lined up on the top shelf, next to a dust-laden bottle of Haig and Haig Pinch. And there was the box of candies next to another box that contained flashlight batteries. Chiang's shop seemed just to fit him, a small closet of commerce.

—I've been here so long now that they don't mention the difference between us any more, he said.

—That's true, Bawang nodded. He swept another candy into his mouth. —And this Chinese is not like the others.

—The Ibans trust me like one of their own, Chiang continued. —I have this shop. I'm a businessman. But really I'm one of them.

He took another candy from the box himself.

—Why are you here, Tuan? he asked.

—Just for a visit.

—But you speak the language so well. You've lived in Sarawak?

—Yes.

—You're sure the government didn't send you?

—Yes. Why?

Chiang grimaced, looking down at the candy wrapper. —The government, they send an officer here sometimes. Every two or three years. The Ibans don't like it. They don't trust the government. Government wants taxes. Government wants them to speak Malay.

Chiang crumpled the wrapper and threw it into the river. The shop was slowly filling with cigarette smoke. A layer of gray mist intermingled with the dry leaves of the fronds in the ceiling, giving Collins the impression that there were soft clouds gathering just above his head.

—The old government, under the English, was better, Tuan, Chiang said, —because they never came here.

Bawang clapped Collins's knee. —I met a white man once, he said, taking a cigarette from Chiang. —At the end of the Japanese war, Tuan. He dropped into the jungle from the air.

—By parachute.

—Yes. He came here with some dark men, different from us.

They were called … what were those men, Chiang? Gokah? Garkah?

Chiang shook his head.

—They said they came from a country where there were high mountains. No jungle.

—Gurkhas, Collins said.

—Something like that, yes. I saw them when they arrived, like orchids floating from the clouds.

Bawang raised his hand and imitated, with his gesture, a parachute dropping to the ground.

—At first I thought it was a dream. They came to help us get rid of the Japanese, he said.

—The Japanese were up here? Collins asked.

—No, they were in Belaga. We took that white man and his friends down there, many of us.

—What happened?

—We brought the Japanese back here.

—All of them?

—No, Tuan, not all of them. Bawang lit his cigarette with the end of Chiang's. —Just part of them.

Collins awaited more explanation. He had not quite followed the last part of the conversation, and wondered whether there were something grammatical, a translation problem maybe, some nuance in Bawang's narrative that he had missed. He looked up at the Iban, puzzled.

—Their heads, Tuan!

The Ibans and Chiang broke into rattling laughter. Ibu's voice soared with high-pitched glee above everyone else's.

—It's true, Bawang said after a moment. —I'll show you. He stepped out on the deck.

A group of Ibans came out of the forest and headed for the notched log ladder that led to the longhouse. The women were dressed in calf-length black cloth, wrapped about their waists. They were bare-breasted, and the rain glimmered darkly against

89

their shoulders and arms. Barefoot, the men wore black loin-cloths. Their black hair hung down about their shoulders. The rainwater brightened the birds and embroidery of their tattoos.

Bawang stood and called to them, as Collins, Chiang, and Ibu joined him on the boat deck. The group halted, amazed by the pale rain-soaked apparition before them. After a moment a few of them descended to the boat, though most remained cautiously where they were. Collins kept quiet, his hands on his waist. His soaked clothing smelled of old sweat. His shoulder bag, as packed with gear as it was, resembled a large slug where it lay on the deck.

The Ibans were dumbfounded. Right away, Collins realized that they had little of the sophistication of the downriver Ibans, who were accustomed to more than a century of English tuans. He knew how these people must feel, recalling the day he had seen his first longhouse and sat down to his first plateful of sago palm worms. There had been in that moment a feeling of real danger. Sago palm worms? Holding one of them between his fingers like a fried thumb, he had not known what to do with it. Subsequent experiences had diminished that fearfulness. But now Collins saw that, for these Ibans at Rumah Nadai, he represented a spectacle, a phantasm. They had heard about people like him on the Iban shortwave radio newscasts for years. Bawang and a few others, evidently, had even seen some during the war. But here, now, they had one, and Collins felt like a yak in the zoo.

—He's going to stay with us a while, Bawang said.

—He's come so far, one of the women muttered. She hunkered on the shore and stared at Collins.

—They never sent anyone like this before, her husband said. He smoked a small handmade pipe that made him appear jaunty despite the heavy load of firewood he carried on his back. —He must be important.

—We shouldn't take this lightly, another, very old woman said. Her skin flapped loosely from her arms, and her breasts hung like two empty wallets. She peered up at Collins as though he might punish her for something. —He may be a bad spirit.

—It is an honor to be here, Collins suddenly said. The Iban words came out with stentorian weight.

The Ibans fell silent.

—I've come to Rumah Nadai to discover for myself ... He held out a hand, gesturing into the forest. —To discover for myself the beauties of upper Rajang and the kindness of the people here.

The utterance, as pompous as it was, was one he had used hundreds of times before, during visits to other longhouses. It invested an arrival with a certain sense of ceremony, as though history were taking place and even possibly being recorded. There had been a time when such a pronouncement had embarrassed Collins and offended his American informality. But he had soon realized that it was expected of him. Just going about your business was rude. No Iban understood such industry. What was needed to show that you were truly sincere was rambling oratory, and this speech dazzled the Ibans.

There was a flurry of excited talk through the rain. This was surely a remarkable man, they said. Not only a tuan, but a tuan we can talk to. Who is he? Where'd he come from?

Bawang took Collins's bag and slung it over his shoulder. Pulled from the boat, Collins stumbled on the bank, falling into the mud. Picking himself up, he went with the Ibans toward Rumah Nadai. The path ran with rain. His shirt stuck to him everywhere.

—Ah, Tuan, Bawang said. Collins's bag swung from his shoulder. He was a muscular man, though quite small. —I'm glad you're here, because I have a question. A question I've had for years.

Swept up in the celebration, Collins looked down at the Iban.

—I listen to the radio at night, you know, the Iban program, Bawang said. —They tell us about the Americans, fighting in a war now in ... where is it?

—Vietnam.

—That's it. And the Americans, they are like the white men, yes?

Collins nodded, knowing that Bawang was talking about the English.

—So they take prisoners, Bawang continued.

The crowd stopped at the notched log leading up to the longhouse. As several Ibans ascended it, Collins waited below with the headman. Bawang was looking up at him, his teeth broadly arranged.

—That's right, Collins said.

—Well, my question is, why do they do that?

Collins pondered the headman a moment. —Because we feel that the soldiers on the other side are fighting for a government that's gone wrong, I guess, but that the soldiers themselves, if they're captured, don't deserve to be killed.

Collins's answer sounded rather leaden, though it was what he believed.

—But Tuan, Bawang said, shaking his head. —They're the enemy.

—It doesn't matter. We shouldn't kill them.

—Why not?

—Because they're human beings, and they surrendered freely.

—Ah. Bawang looked down at the mud below the house. —But ... His face took on a look of genuine puzzlement. —But the Ibans think that, in any battle, we should kill the ones we capture.

—Why?

—Because they were against us.

He gestured toward the log, and Collins began his ascent to the longhouse. He removed his hat. Many of the women who had been working on the porch inside remained seated, stoic in their survey of Collins's legs, his arms, his hair, his enormous presence. But he could tell that, at least for the moment, they were stunned by his sudden arrival.

—Those, for instance, Bawang said. He pointed at the ceiling.

A large basket hung from the ridgepole. It was made of jute, and held more than a dozen skulls that faced out at every angle. The eyes were closed, the skin almost black, most of them retaining their hair. They had been hanging in the basket for many years, judging from the dust and cobwebs that covered them.

—These are the Japanese I told you about, Tuan, Bawang said.

There was no indication in the skulls' faces of the horror of the end of their lives. They appeared peaceful, as though death and dismemberment were like an afternoon nap in a hammock, filled with pleasant dreams. Collins stared at them a long while, not noticing the silence that had spread across the porch. The basket was motionless. Collins's mind wandered as he imagined one of the skulls in life, giving orders, organizing a bivouac or something out in the jungle ... Sergeant Nakamura, maybe, whose wife and kids were in Kyoto. Perhaps he had been a machinist before the war, something like that.

—If we had taken them prisoner, they might have escaped, Bawang said, looking up at the skulls. He lowered hs head, shaking it. —And then we'd have to put up with them all over again.

Bawang waved his hand, then pointed up the long porch. The gesture was magnanimous, taking it all in.

—But in any case, welcome to Rumah Nadai, Tuan, he said. —This is your home now for as long as you wish.

Collins did not reply. He stood looking up at the skulls. He swallowed, but the saliva would not go down his throat. Dust caked Sergeant Nakamura's eyelids.

Over the following months, Collins listened every night to the news broadcasts on Radio Sarawak for word of himself. He felt his absence must be of concern to the consulate people—an officer having disappeared without a word. He often came to a halt, far off in the woods with Bawang, certain that he had heard the familiar drone of American English just beyond the next tree. He would hold out a hand for quiet and look anxiously into the forest. But he saw nothing. No short sleeves and ties. Nothing. And there was no word on the radio, in any of the languages in which the news was broadcast. Collins was offended.

As they listened to the Phillips shortwave that Chiang had brought from Sibu years earlier, Bawang studied the American's face. He was interested in everything Collins did, especially the way the American moved about so nervously, heatedly even, yet with such sloppy motions. Collins turned the dial through splin-

6

ters of voice and music, through Radio Hanoi, Radio Peking, and the BBC World Report, until he arrived at the Malay news. It amused Bawang that Collins cared so little for any of the other stations. As Collins raced through them, the Iban chortled at his frustration.

—Is the information the same, Tuan? he asked one night as Collins switched from the news in Iban to the news in Malay, then to the news in English.

—No. The Malay broadcast talks about the government and how proud they are of it, Collins replied.

Bawang shook his head, disgruntled.

—But, of course, so does the Iban broadcast, Collins continued.

—They have to, Tuan, Bawang nodded. —The government pays them. But they're downriver Ibans anyway. He reached for the small straw basket that hung from the belt of his loincloth. —They have no judgment.

Collins arrived at the Voice of America.

—That's your language, Tuan?

—Yes.

—What do they talk about?

Collins leaned close to the radio.

—In domestic news today, the announcer said, —First Lady Lady Bird Johnson appeared at Bloomingdale's department store in New York City to officially open the Christmas shopping season.

The two men listened for a few minutes, until the announcer turned to news about the Pittsburgh Steelers.

—The same, Collins replied. —The government.

Bawang nodded. He took a pouch of tobacco from the basket and began rolling a cigarette. Intent on the task, he listened to the broadcast a moment, then lit the cigarette and handed it to Collins.

—Tuan, I don't think you look so well.

95

Collins pulled the cigarette from his lips and frowned. He passed it back to the Iban.

—You've lost weight since you got here. Your skin … Bawang placed a finger on Collins's left cheek, next to his eye. —It looks old. I think … I think it doesn't do well in this place. Too much water, maybe.

He pointed at Collins's beard.

—And this, Bawang said, —there's so much of it!

Collins had forgotten to bring along a razor, and he did not want to shave the way the Ibans did, plucking the few whiskers from their chins one by one. So his beard had flourished like a graying shrub.

—And I understand it can be very cold where you come from, Bawang continued.

—Yes, sometimes.

—That the rain is cold.

—Yes.

Bawang drew once more on the cigarette. —I heard that on the radio, too, he said. —There was an Iban on the broadcast, who had gone to England. He said there's no jungle there.

—That's right.

—They have trees, I guess.

—Here and there.

Bawang shook his head. —Barbarous, he muttered. —How can you live without a jungle?

He knocked the gray ash from the end of his cigarette with an index finger.

—Is that why the white men left Borneo? he asked —They didn't like the heat?

Collins leaned his head against the post next to him. —No. They left because they had lost control of their empire.

Bawang observed the end of the cigarette a long while. His face moved with his thoughts, which appeared to arrive at a moment's frustration as his lips ground against each other.

—What did you say? he asked.

Collins had used an Iban phrase that approximated a group of longhouses or part of the river. He did not know the Iban word for empire. He wasn't sure there was one. Bawang's eyes looked up at him with ingenuous interest, and Collins wondered if he could even describe the scope of British holdings, or the purpose of them.

—The white men ... uh, the English ... ruled the world, Collins said. —That's why they were here in the first place.

—They ruled everything?

—Almost.

—The afterworld? The underworld, too?

—No, not those.

Bawang shrugged, not quite understanding. —I've wondered about that, he said. —I thought there must be some kind of magic power here that they wanted

—In a way ...

—They must not have been very good rulers, Tuan.

—Why?

—Because they came here, stayed for a hundred years, and left, and we never saw them.

Collins began laughing.

—When we Ibans take over another part of the river, Bawang continued, —we make sure they know who we are.

—But the English were like that elsewhere, Collins replied. —Sometimes they fought big wars against other countries to make sure they kept what they'd gotten.

—Against the Japanese, you mean, Bawang said.

—Especially against the Japanese.

—I'm glad they did. We were happy to see the English come back. The Japanese never understood how to run this place.

—Even though they're Asians?

Bawang puzzled a moment. —What's that, Tuan? An Asian.

—Asians are all the people who live in this part of the world.

They ... they ... Collins stumbled over the explanation.
—Bawang, you're an Asian!

—No, I'm an Iban.

—But the Ibans are Asians. The Japanese are Asians.

Bawang nodded. —Maybe so. But just because we're neighbors doesn't seem to matter. I know the English come from far across many oceans. But I've heard from downriver that you can at least talk to the English. The Japanese ... He harrumphed, shaking his head. —The Japanese. The phrase ended with a grumbling sigh.

Through all the years he had been working in Sarawak, Collins had been waiting for some indication from some Iban somewhere of political anger toward the English intruders. But it had never come. Collins himself thought that colonialization of any kind was an evil. It was part of his idea of himself as an American. Sure, you go out there to help people. And then, he thought, you leave. But he had to admit that the protestations he had heard from his British friends—that that was a lot of bloody rot, Dan, that we see what you aim to do in Vietnam—were unsettling.

But the Ibans had loved the English. Collins had long ago decided that they must have received a kind of respect from the English that was not forthcoming from the Malays, who now ran the government, or the Chinese, who had forever run the economy.

—Why couldn't you run the place? Collins asked.

—The Ibans? Bawang asked. —We did! He put his cigarette out on the bottom of his foot. Dropping the butt through a crack in the floor, he pulled his knees up toward his chest. He was an inquiring man, and Collins had come to expect unusual answers from him.

—We always did, he continued. —For us up here, the white men were like oracles or spirits. They lived in Kuching, far away, and dispensed ... dispensed ... He searched for the word. —Wisdom! But up here we did what we wanted.

—So you liked them?

—Of course. For instance, the English would tell us what to do. And we knew about that because every now and then someone would come up here to say that there was a new head white man or that there was a new law or something. And that was the last we'd ever hear of it. But the Japanese actually required us to do what they said, and that was the difference.

—I see.

—And that's why, when they left, we treated them so differently from the way we treated the English when they left.

Collins shuddered.

But there never was anything about Collins on the news broadcasts. It's like I vanished, he thought, until he realized that that was precisely what had happened. He wished he could be pleased that no one was looking for him. But he found that he *wanted* to be the object of a search. He wanted the opportunity to explain what he had done, and why.

Collins did not feel he had just gone native, which was an expression filled with contempt. It made "native" sound like a state of debased moral emptiness. There was truly a colonialist feel to the term. On one side, a decorous state of civilization, something grand and silent and organized, stood guard. The Court of Saint James. Monticello. That kind of thing. On the other side, the rest—the churlish mud, the comic desperation of so many villages rickety with dried-out thatch, the deterioration and constant fecundity, the thousands of languages, animal shit everywhere, and the fall of water down blue jungle gorges—that was native. To Queen Victoria or at least to Joe Feeney, going there meant an abandonment of the desirable, the civilized, the truth.

For a while Collins decided that, really, he was involved in a protest. The State Department had implemented an unfair policy. That was it. They were victimizing their own people and those they had trained to help. But Collins's self-righteousness suffered from the reemergence of his own State Department training. He had been as good a bureaucrat as the next fellow. Often, even he thought his running into the mountains was just unprofessional behavior.

So it was that dismay began to subtly slip into his feelings, without provocation. As his clothes grew dirtier, as he began to have to mend them, as his hair became shaggy and his feet began to wrinkle from the ravages of the damp, he worried that he had simply abandoned himself. The State Department doesn't care because they know I'll come back into Kuching one day myself, to ask their forgiveness. All they have to do is wait. And they won't forgive me.

As the months passed, Collins became rather used-looking. His skin roughened and, in places, got spongey with rough-edged holes. The edges of his heels hardened and then cracked, quite painfully. There was no medication, so he simply had to grow accustomed to the pain. He limped around for a few months, then forgot about it.

During the five minutes before bed every night, he surveyed himself for injuries and bites. In the first week, he was bitten by a small centipede, and the welt that was left behind stayed with him for a month. The centipede tried to scurry away, but Collins retaliated with the flat bottom of one of his sandals.

He cut himself now and then, which normally would not be a problem. In the jungle, however, with its rain and constant heat, the cuts would not heal. They oozed for weeks. Chiang had an ancient, rusted tin of band-aids that he gave Collins. Despite these, the flies would not leave him alone. They congregated around a wound, easily evading Collins's hand waving about above it. Scrapes and abrasions were the same, as were skin-burns, like the one Collins got when he fell down a wet boulder one day, leaving a raspberry on his leg. For a few weeks after that, he led a squadron of flies around the longhouse and the woods.

Sometimes, Collins felt he could see undulations in the ground cover, caused by the mountainous quantities of bugs. And they all seemed, at one time or another, to find him. The first centipede informed him of the presence of such things. But then he found that there were legions of that particular centipede, as well as many others. There were brown ones, gold ones, yellow and red ...

Then, there were snakes. The one he knew about already—the black and yellow striped krait—was famous throughout Borneo for its deadly venom. But there were other kraits, differently colored. There were also spiders, bees, and a particularly virulent-looking kind of cockroach that, happily for Collins, was harmless. But it reminded him of a recurrent dream he had had as a child, in which he was chased about by a phantasm that oozed, from its pus-imbued skin, a foamy, black spittle.

Because of all these, Collins was quite careful about his mosquito net. Chiang had given him one that he hung from a rafter over his sleeping mat. While the Ibans rolled their nets up every morning, Collins kept his down, the bottom of it tucked in around the mat itself, all day. He wanted no entry of any creature that could wake him up, just to enjoy the view from his forehead. So he carefully checked the net each morning. Then, each night, he checked it again.

One evening, he sat up late with Chiang, listening to the radio. Collins translated the program for him, a BBC production that had to do with the proper care of motorcycles. Chiang had seen a motorcycle once many years before, on his only trip to Kuching, so he was interested in what the radio had to say. The single part of the broadcast he really understood was the description of the spark plug. He understood what a spark plug was, and he laughed, slapping his knee, when Collins translated the announcer's advice for what to do when a spark plug got wet.

—Oh, I know, Tuan, he grinned. —I have seen that happen. But at least with a motorcycle, you stop when such a disaster strikes. In a boat, you keep going. The rapids take you. You capsize.

As the porch emptied, Collins grew sleepy, and he excused himself to go to bed. He entered the room he shared with Bawang's family. The lowered mosquito nets hung about the different sleeping mats, like gauze pillars. Collins made his way to his own, listening to the breathing in the room. Holding his candle up to inspect his net, he saw that it was clear of any bugs. Mosquitoes flew about him in a droning cloud, and he slapped at one that landed on his ear. He placed the candle holder on the floor, removed his shorts, and parted the net just wide enough to sneak inside. Kneeling on his mat, he reached a hand outside the net for the candle.

There was a movement to his left. Startled, Collins sat back and looked up over his shoulder. A scorpion, hanging from a corner of the net, readied itself for an attack.

It was a very, very large scorpion. Its tail curved up over its head and quivered. Collins moved away. He sensed the scorpion's anger, as its eyes seemed to expand and fix on him. Indeed, Collins moved away so quickly that he almost pulled the mosquito net down on his head.

The scorpion began to move down the netting toward him. Its tail jerked back and forth as it struggled with its footing. Collins hurried from the net and retreated to a corner of the room, where Bawang kept a carved walking stick. He took it up and carefully reentered the mosquito net. Extending the stick toward the scorpion, he coaxed it onto the far end.

The scorpion looked like the potato bugs he had victimized as a little boy, though it was a far more sleek-looking creature. As it stared down the stick at Collins, its tail beginning to rise up over its head again, Collins realized it was also more aggressive than the potato bug. The scorpion took a step toward the American. Slowly, with a rickety movement like a dump truck coasting down a rutted track, it made its way.

Collins tried holding the stick away from himself, as though the increased distance would tire the bug. He did not want to shake the stick, for fear that the scorpion would drop off it into his bedding. But the scorpion would be upon him in a minute or so, and it refused to stop, despite Collins's firm order to do so.

Collins backed out from beneath the netting, holding the stick up at an angle. He backed toward the kitchen, pursued inexorably by the scorpion, which appeared to be sweating. Its quivering gave it the appearance of gleefulness. Collins tripped, but caught himself with one hand on a wooden pillar. The scorpion paused a moment, as though to see whether the American were all right. Sensing that he had recovered himself, it moved on.

Collins turned and hurried with the stick into the kitchen. The scorpion arrived at his thumb and examined it. Collins cried out, his voice rising to a quivering scream. The tail shook in an erect spasm. Collins thrust the stick out the back entry and dropped it to the ground below.

His heart staggered. He leaned against the palm-frond wall in the kitchen, then sensed that there were other bugs ... lots of them ... crawling about in the wall itself. He jumped away. He took his breath in gulps. He hurried toward the safety of his netting, then halted, wondering whether it were really safe. As well, he imagined the scorpion down below the house in the mud, looking for a way to get back into the room, so that it could look once more for the funny man with the stick.

The following morning, Collins was sitting on the outside porch of the house when he saw a pillar of black smoke rising over the forest. He stood and walked to the end of the porch, for a moment fearful that fire had broken out at a house upriver. But no one else working on the porch appeared alarmed, and Bawang, who had been sharpening a *parang* knife, explained that some Ibans up there were just preparing a hillside for rice planting.

—We'll all be doing it soon enough, Bawang muttered, shaking his head.

—You don't care for it? Collins asked.

A long exhalation passed through Bawang's tightened lips.

—It's just a lot of work, he said. —You come home from a day on the hillside, and all you want to do is lie down in the river. Maybe let the river take you away.

—I can help you, Bawang. I'm good with a shovel.

The Iban shook his head. —This isn't work for a tuan.

—Why not?

—Tuans are in charge of things. They're kings. They rule. There was a note of irony in Bawang's reply, fun at the expense of the tuans' view of themselves.

—Bawang, take me out there and teach me how to do it, Collins grumbled.

Bawang shrugged and agreed.

A few days later, they went out with a half dozen other men from the house, along a trail that followed the river a few miles into some small hills. The hills had once been cleared of jungle, but that was years before. Now they were covered with gnarled scrub and trees.

—I planted here about five years ago, I think, Bawang said. —The soil's ready again.

He dug with his hand into the dirt, pulling up some black mud.

—So now all we have to do is clear this slash away. Bawang gestured up the hill. —And we'll have enough rice for a year.

Collins looked up the slope. He held a *parang* in his hand, as did all the men. As it happened, there were no shovels.

By the end of the day, Collins had felled a dozen small trees, a task that had blistered his hands and made his arms feel jellied and insubstantial. But that had been the easy part. More difficult was to remove the stumps from the hillside. Digging into the soil with their *parangs*, the men grasped the stumps with their hands and wrestled them from the ground. With most stumps, they wrestled for quite some time. By two in the afternoon, when it became too hot to work any longer, they went down to the river to wash.

Collins had some trouble getting into the river, since he had to climb down rocks that required him to use his hands. Then, getting back out of the river was difficult because his back hurt so much. He decided to stay in the water for a while.

Finally, the Ibans helped him up the bank, and after their siesta he spent the afternoon watching them work.

The following day, Collins was back. He wrapped his hands in some cloth Bawang had given him and, despite the tight aches in most of his muscles, he went to work. He could not do as much as he had done the day before, but the Ibans let him carry a lot of the slash and stumps to the bonfires, which burned all day. Smoke swirled into the air and all across the hillside. Bawang had warned Collins about the smoke, and the American had brought along another shirt to tie across his face as a mask. By the end of the second day, he was as fatigued as he had been the day before, and blackened with soot. A few of his blisters had opened up, and blood oozed here and there from the black grit of his skin.

He lay in the river again.

The third day he went out to the site, but heeded Bawang's advice not to do any work.

—You can use the rest, I think, Tuan, Bawang said as he trudged up the hill toward the last stand of trees.

The fourth day, Collins returned once more. He had known, the day previous, that he should rest. But he had been embarrassed by his inactivity. He felt he had to prove himself in some way. If tuans were so important, they should be able to pull their share of the load, he thought.

These people were feeding him and offering him shelter. It seemed only right that he be able to carry some few hundred damned stumps ... He sighed to himself as his gaze wandered up the moonlike slope, now black, gray, and smoldering in the dawn sunlight.

Collins was as tired as he had ever been.

By the end of the day, the entire hillside was cleared, and the fires burning along the top ridge seemed celebratory in their hellish noise. Black smoke—the result of the talkative industry of Collins's companions and of his own painful efforts—rose into the air and dispersed hundreds of feet up, drifting over the river and out of sight beyond the tree canopy. Collins sat at the edge of the field. He was once again blackened and dazed. But the fire served to cleanse him of his pain and complaint. The shoots of rice would go into the ground within a few days, and he looked forward to that.

The Ibans showed Collins everything they knew. How to cull rice. Where to bury a woman's afterbirth. The way to prepare the dead for burial, with turmeric and cleansed wrappings. How to cook pig. They explained the rain to him, that, if you noticed, the storms in the dry season were a different color from those during the monsoon. They explained which colors they were, and why.

Collins learned to fish. The Ibans used a kind of trap with a wooden frame and netting that they placed at higher spots in the river, above the riffles. Collins suggested a different sort of door latch that allowed the fish to enter more easily. This advance secured Collins's place in the longhouse because it finally proved he could serve a purpose.

But that was more important to Collins than it was to the Ibans. They were pleased to have him in the house no matter what he did. No outsider other than Chiang had ever had such regard for them. Indeed they frequently referred to him as "Tuan Chiang's brother," since both men took so readily to the Iban ways of doing things. Chiang had coined the term, saying "you come from the outside to this place, Tuan, you must be ready to make some changes."

—Maybe you should become Chinese, Chiang had added, —so that you can become Iban, like me.

One night, Collins had a dream of a hornbill bird flying through the forest and disappearing in a rain mist that clung to a hillside. The cloud began to glow from inside. At first, the light took the shape and colors of the hornbill's beak, which was curved, very long, red and glaring green. Soon, flames broke out on the cloud's surface, dark as spurts of burning blood. Collins explained the next morning how the dream had frightened him and how glad he was that such things did not really occur.

—But it did occur, Bawang said, shaking his head and looking about. He was a *lemambang,* a religious man who was able to tell the American how crops could be insured and babies could be guaranteed good health. He explained that warriors killed in battle were ushered into the celestial forest on the wings of spirit hornbills.

—Just in the dream, though, Collins replied.

—It's all the same. You've seen how the wind can turn cold in a minute, as though it were breathed by a ghost. You know how the roots will reach out to twist your ankle, Tuan. It's the same. The same spirits visit during the day as during the night.

Bawang wrapped his hands together.

—There's no difference. Watch out for that mist, he said.

The Ibans showed him how to dance.

—Do you know the *gamelan,* Tuan? Chiang asked one night as they prepared for the planting festival. Since the hillsides had been cleared and the slash burnt away, all that remained was the festival to insure the crop's success. There had been so much activity in the longhouse during the day that the anticipation of music and a party incited great frivolity up and down the porch, anxious, crying children, and early drinking. Collins and Chiang sat at a mat, having a snack of cooked pork and rice.

—I've done it, Collins replied.

—You have?

—I went to a longhouse in the Second Division once. A place called Long Ili. They set up the gongs and the *gamelan,* and they wanted me to …

Collins extended his arms behind him and cocked his head to the side, turning his upper body about at an angle.

—To do the hornbill dance? Chiang asked. He slapped the mat, a broad grin on his face. Lantern light was reflected in the sweat of his forehead. He beckoned toward Bawang, who remained intent on helping several women set up the musical instruments.

—All I did was play one of the gongs, Collins continued. —The big one. So it required … He took up a slice of pork and flipped it into his mouth. —It required little talent.

—Did you dance?

—No.

—Why not?

A shadowy cloud moved through Collins's heart as he recalled his hesitation that evening at Long Ili. He remembered how much he had wanted to join in the dance. But he had been visiting the place with Tully Spencer, and the idea of his moving about the longhouse porch, gong music humming deeply through his gut as he imitated the fine flight of the hornbill through the higher world … that idea had fallen prey to Spencer's stuffy disapproval. It wouldn't do, an AID man, dancing like that. It just wouldn't do.

So he hadn't.

Chiang beckoned to Bawang once more. —You know, the tuan here has never done the hornbill. He turned to Collins a moment. —You've seen it, though?

—Many times.

—The dance of the heavenly bird. It graces the longhouse with its flight.

—Of course.

—A warrior who can do that dance is the best kind of person, because he's brave, he takes heads, *and* he's a graceful man as well. He's cruel. Quick. And even beautiful when his wings pass over the air.

Bawang sat down next to the two men. He had overheard the last few sentences and nodded his approval of Chiang's description.

—It's more important than that, even, Bawang said. —Because he *is* the heavenly bird itself when he dances.

Just then, the *gamelan* began playing, and the porch erupted into talk and amusement. Children gathered about the musicians, their eyes cast up at the large hanging gongs. There was just a single *gamelan*—a bed of curved metal plates lying side to side over a bamboo stand. The musician, an older woman who hunched over the instrument and paid little attention to the surrounding crowd, played it with a crudely cast metal hammer. The precise notes of the *gamelan*, high pitched and fast, were quite playful in comparison with the gongs, which resonated through the porch like dark, constant water.

Suddenly, a figure ran from one of the rooms, a man wearing a long cape of feathered wings and a bird headdress. He ran up and down the porch at first, frightening the children into laughter, his head shaking back and forth and his wings bristling as he imitated a bird's flight. After a moment, the bird began to twirl. Its wings reached out behind, to ride on the upswirl of air as he turned about in time to the gong's rhythms. The crowd on the porch grew quieter, as though they were themselves gliding with him. Collins had seen the Ibans pay this kind of regard to real birds. They often talked about what it would be like to soar like that, to see the forest from up above, beyond the tree canopy in full, blinding light.

The dancer approached Collins and harassed him a bit, standing before him to shake his wings. Collins saw the man's face hidden beneath the headdress, opened up in a smile. The beak, carved from hardwood, came out from above his head and curved down over his eyes. The feathers actually rattled, and dust flew from the costume. It was old, and the feathers appeared to have dried out. They were like brown-yellow fronds laid out in a closely woven design. Parts of the wings were bug-eaten. Indeed, Collins saw that attempts to mend them had themselves fallen apart, so that the bird took on an aged, menacing intensity.

Suddenly, the bird reached down and pulled Collins to his feet. Bawang and Chiang followed, as the bird and Collins hurried across the porch toward one of the longhouse rooms. There was a surge of noisy glee from the crowd, cut off by the door closing behind the men.

—Here, Tuan. Put these on, the dancer said. He pulled the feather costume from his shoulders, helped with it by Bawang. They lifted it up over Collins's head. The American ducked as he felt the costume press down on his shoulders. The costume scratched and weighed him down, like a hairshirt.

—This, too, Bawang said. He placed the headdress over Collins's head. Outside, the *gamelan* played on. The drone of the gongs shivered through the floorboards.

—So let's see you dance. Bawang clapped Collins's shoulder, then moved to the door.

As he emerged onto the porch once more, Collins felt the rattling, dried-out weight of the feathers all around him. Dust blew about, and he sneezed a couple of times. When he tried wiping his nose, the sleeve of feathers collided with his beak, and he could do nothing. He sneezed again.

There was applause as he made his way toward the crowd. Realizing that he would make little impression as a bird just walking along—some kind of jungle penguin—he quickly spread his wings out to the side and began to turn about, approaching the *gamelan* in circles, his body at a tilt. He turned his head back and forth, as though he were in search of a landing place on some high branch. Collins concentrated so much on trying to imitate the movements he had seen others do that he barely saw the audience. He heard their laughter, their clapping and shouting. But he felt entirely graceless.

He imagined how foolish he must look to the Ibans, struggling beneath the wings. He turned about, against the rhythm of the *gamelan,* even stumbling once, yet still turning and turning. He sweat. He tried to feel the spirit of the bird, but he could not. The sense he wished to have, that somehow he was actually flying, was not there. He turned once more, then dropped his arms, shaking his head.

But the *gamelan* continued. Looking out at the crowd, Collins saw that they were indeed taken by his appearance. Bawang and Chiang stood to the side, both men's faces dark in the glooming light. They appeared surprised by Collins's effort, as though they had expected simply to have some fun with him. But Bawang's mouth was open in a look of startled respect. Children stared up at Collins, half fearful, half amused. He shook the wings, and the crowd broke into loud applause. The *gamelan* sputtered through several high notes, and once more—despite the sweat burning his eyes, his back itchy from the close press of the costume—Collins took off.

Collins, for sport, took up the blowgun. He had come to admire Bawang's expertise with the weap-on. Bawang could fell a bird from a branch at fifty yards. The bird, sitting around chirping in a breeze, would suddenly catch a dart in the breast and, still in strangled song, fall branch to branch to the ground. Since Bawang could see the truth of things—the crystalline message to be found in mysterious happenings—it came as no surprise to Collins to learn that he had once even nailed a chicken hawk on the wing. Impossible. Even Chiang, who was an expert with the weapon himself, marveled at Bawang's effortless, almost liquid sense of where he was, and where the birds were, when he hunted.

Bawang gave Collins an old blowgun, about six feet long and perfectly plumbed, that was made of first-growth ironwood. He also gave him some ragged darts.

—They won't fly well, Tuan, he said, fingering one of them. It appeared much used, scratched here and there with some nicks taken out of it. He placed the dart in the blowgun, just inside the mouthpiece. Then, lifting the gun to his lips, he held it up at an angle. Gripping it with both hands just in front of his mouth, he allowed his cheeks to fill with air.

Collins looked up into the trees, in the direction Bawang was facing. He could see nothing but the chaotic undersurface of the tree cover, further confused by hanging vines and mosses. There was a sudden breathy noise, and the dart flew toward the trees. Bawang lowered the gun from his lips and stared up into the forest. The dart had disappeared, and Collins turned toward the Iban, smiling.

—Wow! he said. He waited for Bawang to let him try the blowgun. But Bawang paid no attention.

—Not yet, Tuan, Chiang counseled, whispering. —Wait.

Raising a hand for quiet, Bawang suddenly pointed up above. Collins saw a feathery shadow falling, and Bawang ran off through the undergrowth. By the time Collins and Chiang caught up with him, he had wrung the bird's neck and was securing it to a leather strap around his waist.

—Don't talk after you shoot, Bawang said. He made a sweeping gesture all around him. —You see, it disturbs the trees.

Apologetic, Collins nodded.

—Your turn. Bawang handed the blowgun to Collins.

—I probably won't hit anything, the American said.

—Doesn't matter. It was years before Chiang could.

—It was? Collins glanced at Chiang.

—Yes, he could aim in whatever direction, at the entire forest, and still miss everything, Bawang said.

Collins knew that Chiang made the best darts in the entire house. They flew true every time. So the American was heartened by the idea that Chiang had once been a feckless amateur too.

—Okay, then, Collins whispered. He placed a dart in the gun and raised the weapon to his lips. Filling his cheeks with air, he attempted to hold the gun steady. But the far end of it wavered about like a clock's pendulum. He let the breath out of his cheeks, lowered the blowgun, then raised it once more to his lips.

Gathering himself, he blew into the gun and awaited the dart's flight. But nothing happened. Muttering, Collins lowered the gun again. He lifted it before him to examine it. He shook it up and down. The dart slid down its length and dribbled to the ground.

—That's a lucky bird up there on that branch, Bawang nodded.

A few days later, Chiang took Collins aside to a bamboo chicken coop he kept several yards upriver from the house. He wanted their visit to be kept secret, gesturing behind himself for Collins to walk carefully, to make no noise. Puzzled, Collins stepped silently through the twigs and mud. The chicken coop was one of many that were sheltered beneath a palm-frond lean-to, fenced all around for protection from the longhouse's dogs.

Chiang's head was wrapped in a piece of black cotton, and he wore a loincloth. His hands were soiled, weather-beaten by his work in the fields. He looked over his shoulder several times secretively. Collins looked back at the longhouse once himself. No one was watching them.

—Here, Tuan. Look at this, Chiang whispered.

He opened the bamboo latch to one of the chicken coops, reached inside, looked over his shoulder once again, and pulled out an intense, lean, finely feathered fighting cock.

—I wanted you to see this. Just you, Chiang continued whispering. He hunkered down on the ground, grooming the bird as it jerked its head back and forth. —I don't know how much you know about the cockfights.

Collins shook his head. —Well, I've seen some, you know, some …

He let the phrase wander to silence. He was too distracted by the bird's remarkable beauty to even speak. It was a handsome and humorous fighting cock, red-brown, with a quick turn of the head. Its wattle was long, and burgundy-colored. The American figured he was being given some sort of preview of Chiang's new champion.

—You *should* learn about them, Chiang said. —Because with a bird like this one, you could be an important man here. More important than you are already.

113

—Maybe so. But it takes time to breed birds. And knowledge …

—You don't have to worry about that, Tuan.

Collins looked up from the bird. Chiang's face suddenly opened up as his eyes brightened.

—Because he's yours, Chiang said.

—Mine! Collins said. —Why?

There was a quick storm of clucking and sharply beating wings.

—I have other ones, Chiang replied, holding his head back to avoid the flapping feathers. —And you can learn about the cockfights with this bird. How to handle them.

The bird calmed itself.

—And I just wanted to give you something as a gift, for the way you've tried to go about things here. I know how difficult it is, to be a stranger, to speak some other language. I know how lonely you can get up here, Tuan, listening to that radio every night.

—But …

—Besides, it makes the people laugh, how you try to do things you've never done before. The way they laughed at me so long ago. And I liked it then, because it showed how they felt about me. How kind they were.

The bird flapped noisily once more.

—Even though the Ibans are like everyone else, you know, Chiang continued. —They have divorce and insincerity. Madness. Cruel people. People who talk too much, or don't understand anything. They have all those, just like the Chinese. Just like, maybe …

Chiang held out his hand, palm up.

—Do the Americans have such things?

Collins nodded.

—But for the most part the Iban heart is good, Chiang continued, —and they'll help you.

He passed the cock to Collins, who gripped it between his hands, fearful it would fly away.

—No, Tuan, not like that, Chiang cautioned. —You'll crush him if you hold him so tight.

Chiang rearranged the bird between Collins's hands.

—He might go after *you* if you treat him that way, instead of after some other rooster, Chiang said, releasing the bird once more into Collins's now softer hold. —And you don't want that, especially if he's got the spurs on.

The fighting cock seemed to calm down as Collins held him. His head snapped right to left, yet Collins felt for a moment that the bird was soothed by his touch, until suddenly it jumped from his hands and flapped into the air. Collins chased after him.

—You're lucky I just trimmed his wings, Chiang shouted as Collins pursued the bird beneath the longhouse. The bird appeared to ricochet between the pilings. The chase scattered a trio of small pigs that were lying in the shaded mud.

Later, sitting on the longhouse porch outside, Collins studied the bird more carefully. Something that had moved Collins's heart even as a child, that had made him want to be a scientist or a spaceship pilot or something, was simply the way things fit together. Even in the second grade, Collins had seen that the world was not a chaotic place. It had glorious beauties, in the way anenomes gather themselves like sagging flowers on the inter-tidal rocks or seagulls appear so efficiently sleek gliding low across a mudflat. Or the mudflat itself, its watery meanders finely curved and lazy in such dark grays.

He watched his new bird cluck about, and marveled at the perfect organization of his feathers—the colors they held, for one thing. This was no washed-out, listless chicken. The brown of his feathers had a glow of almost golden brightness, luminescent in the direct sunlight. About his neck and, especially in the topknot springing from his head, darker red feathers added a kind of reserve to the bird's beauty, a reminder that there was authority in him, that he was not just a pretty-boy.

The bird drew immediate praise from the Ibans. Bawang confided in Collins that he had gotten something very special.

—Chiang's careful with his chickens. He doesn't have any bad ones, Bawang said. —So, no matter what he gives you, you'll have a chance to win a fight or two.

And Collins saw that such a fighting cock could indeed help him in the longhouse. A man with a championship bird has special talents—good *ubat,* as the Ibans called it—a kind of remarkable aura. And he felt that if he, an outsider, could win some fights with this bird, he could enhance his reputation with the Ibans. Maybe join Chiang in the inner circle someday. The bird was small, but intensely fiery. Its eyes flicked about. It preened and cast an eye downward on the other birds, and its clucking sounded like cocky laughter.

Collins named him Harry Truman.

Chiang set up some private training sessions, far from the longhouse. The two men took Harry into the forest, and Chiang began by advising the American how most calmly to prepare the bird so there would be no accidents.

—First, there are the spurs, of course, he said. He took a pair of them, wrapped in their own rattan strings, from a cloth bag. They were tiny, curved knives that had been carefully polished. He handed them to Collins.

—And you have to watch out because they're very sharp, Chiang cautioned.

He took a leaf from a bamboo plant and gave it to the American. Collins ran one of the blades through the leaf, and the two sliced pieces fell quietly to the ground.

—That could be your gut, Tuan, Chiang said. —So be careful.

With the rattan, Chiang attached the spur to the back portion of Harry's right foot. He removed the spur, then demonstrated the process again, showing Collins how to hold the bird in such a way that it could make no sudden movements. Once, Harry objected, demanding with a flurry of squawks that he be left alone, and both men flinched. Especially Collins, who imagined his hand carved into pieces by the Zorro-quick slice of Harry's anger.

—And you have to be sure they'll stay on during a fight, Tuan, Chiang said. He removed the blades and replaced them in his bag. —Because there's nothing he can do to help himself if the spurs come loose.

Next, Chiang taught Collins how to incite the bird to violence.

The two men squatted, facing each other. They had tethered Harry, and he scratched and pecked at the ground a few yards away.

—You hold him out front, like this, Chiang said. He extended his empty hands while Collins watched.

—Come on. You do it, too, Chiang prodded.

Collins held his hands out.

—And you push the birds toward each other. You've seen it.

Collins recalled the way a bird's neck feathers would bristle as he was forced to confront an opponent. Chiang raised his hands again, then once more, as did Collins. Finally, they opened their hands, letting the imaginary birds fly up against each other, their feet seeking the other's chest.

—Now, the important thing to remember, Chiang said, —is that a bird can feel how you feel. If you're nervous, he'll be nervous. If you're calm, he will be, too. So be collected, Tuan. Gather yourself before the fight. Think of the result, your bird triumphant over the body of his gasping opponent. The champion, perhaps, ... wounded, in pain and bloodied ...

Chiang acted out the moment he had just described, cocking his head with self-satisfaction.

—But alive, he said. —The winner!

Quickly he glanced up at Collins, and a pleasureful smile spread across his face.

On Chiang's advice, Collins held Harry back from the first tournament in which he could have fought. Collins wanted to enter Harry, but Chiang counseled that a fight too early in a bird's career could ruin his confidence.

—And yours, as well, Chiang said. —No, you should watch one first, Tuan. But watch it from the point of view of a participant. See how the men handle themselves. See what happens.

So, Collins and Harry sat the tournament out. On the appointed day, the Ibans gathered about the ring, a simple open space several yards from the house. Though it had rained during the night, the sun shined clearly through the forest canopy, spraying the ring with dappled coins of light. It was a very warm morning. Collins's back dripped with sweat as he made his way with Chiang through the gathering of tribespeople, many of whom carried birds of their own, others—both men and women —making wagers, still others drinking large amounts of *tuak* wine. The betting had begun even before sunup, a number of the Ibans standing about in the darkness disputing the birds' athleticism ... this one's quickness, that one's tenacity, and so on. Chiang talked constantly, pointing out to the American how different all the birds were from each other. He had a bookie's knowledge of chicken flesh, and he gave Collins a storm of information.

First there was the speed of a flapping wing. —See that, Tuan? That's spirit. Lots of spirit. Then there was the way a bird returns a glance. The sense of calm or of anxiety, and the way those states of mind change as the moment to fight approaches. Listening intently, Collins found himself dizzied by the sheer amount of advice Chiang gave him. There was lineage, chicken lineage. Owner lineage. Weight. Quickness. Spunk.

The men carried their birds in their hands like jeweled, velvet boxes. They cared for them so well that the ultimate purpose of the birds' lives seemed barely possible. The birds were like gifts fashioned for beauty, finely made and elegant in their calm. Not at all instruments of carnage.

The betting was constant and noisy. Some of the bettors hid their money, as though they feared they might be taken by a shill. Others waved their few *ringgit* about in the air and yelled out what they were willing to bet. They berated anyone who would not take a wager, and laughed at the foolishness of one bird and the cowardice of the next. Everywhere there was chaotic talk and dirty, crumpled bills.

Bawang joined Chiang and Collins. —Luck means everything, he said as they watched several men in a group tying spurs onto the feet of their birds. —It seems to follow some birds right through to the end of a fight.

One of the men, a slim Iban in a pair of tattered long pants, looked up at Collins. Kanong was his name. He had suffered from smallpox as a child, and his face was covered with dark craters. He was embarrassed by his appearance, frequently referring to the disfiguring disease. It appeared to Collins that he would hide his face if he could.

—That's right, Kanong nodded. —And it has a lot to do with who the owner is, don't you think, Bawang?

He cinched one of the spurs tight, then began putting on the second one. His bird had a shiny brown hue and a black wattle. He was excitable, and seemed distracted by the attention being paid to him.

—Down at Rumah Anting last year, for instance, Kanong continued, —I saw a very tough-minded cock, a real bantam, Tuan, ready to take on anything ...

His bird began flapping its wings, and the Iban held him close to calm him down.

—And I saw that bird lose. And I knew ahead of time that it would, because its owner went about shaking his head all morning before the fight.

He wrapped the rattan cord around his bird's foot.

—Convinced it was an underdog, eh? Bawang observed, chuckling.

—That's it, Kanong replied sadly. He shook his head. —Some people ... He looked away from his bird a moment and surveyed the ground. —Some people are like that.

Bawang nodded. —It's true, Tuan. Luck is simply unforgiving, sometimes. So illusory a thing. Just something in the air, you know. And cruel.

—Luck, Kanong interjected, shaking his head. —It can even ferret out a phony. In fact, it usually does.

—Because false bravado goes nowhere, see? If a softhearted owner suddenly begins talking about the murderous instincts of his bird, everyone knows that the bird has little chance of winning. If at all, a man like that wins with a bird capable of guile. But usually he loses.

—Why? Collins asked.

120   Kanong checked the binding on his bird's feet.

—Because not many chickens ...

The bird squawked, then settled down once more, allowing Kanong to continue looking him over.

—Because not many chickens have a sense of strategy, Tuan, he continued. The spurs were perfectly tied. —You'll find that out.

Kanong uttered his last remark as though he wished Collins could avoid such a difficult lesson. The American awaited a further explanation, but none came.

Bawang was to referee the tournament, and he excused himself to call up the first fight. The two contestants entered the ring, and one of them was Kanong. His bird was to fight against that of his cousin Michael. The families of the two men lived in adjoining rooms in the house. Michael was a young, rather portly man, one of the Ibans with whom Collins had toiled to clear the hillside. Bawang had explained that he was born when the Australians were here, and so was named after one of them. The men entered the

ring from opposite sides and approached Bawang in the center. Bawang explained a few rules, and then the men hunkered down. Each held his bird up before him to taunt the opponent. At Bawang's sign, the men let the two birds go.

They immediately jumped up against each other, flailing their wings and squawking. The moment was actually comic, the fury of the opponents made laughable by their manic clucking. But the spurs flashed in the light and, right away, Kanong's bird was hit.

Immediately the wounded warrior turned and ran to the edge of the ring. But its foe would not let it escape. The birds struggled once more into the ring, into the clear, one terrorizing the other. Kanong picked up the wounded cock and carried it to safety.

The bird died even as Kanong pushed his way through the crowd. Collins followed him beyond the ring, away from the spectators. Kanong's hands glimmered with the cock's blood. Within a few seconds, the bird was sagging in his hands, and now it lay there, its head swinging toward the ground. Kanong seemed despondent. Everything had happened so quickly that there had been no anticipation of instantaneous death, and Kanong's eyes glistened black with surprised defeat.

Finally, three weeks later, the day came for Harry to fight. Collins had been living at Rumah Nadai for about half a year, and his presence in the forest was well known. But he had not met many of the Ibans from other houses. So this tournament, to which several neighboring houses had been invited, was to be a kind of introduction as well. Everyone would get a chance to see who this white man was.

Collins awoke, quite nervous, at about three in the morning. He tried to calm himself, but the uncertainty of what would happen to Harry, about how he would do, kept Collins turning about beneath his mosquito net. At last, the forest birds began their pre-dawn singing, a looping, lyrical cacophony, and Collins felt justified in getting up.

Chiang was waiting for him. —Get dressed, Tuan. Wash yourself. We've got to get busy, he said.

By the time Collins had put on a pair of shorts, there was enough light to see the cockfight ring. Several Ibans he did not recognize were standing about talking. When Collins came out of the house with Chiang, there was general quiet as the strangers surveyed the white man. They had heard about him, but this first glimpse of him, descending from the house with Harry cradled in one arm, unsettled them nonetheless.

At first, no one volunteered his bird to fight Harry. Collins worried that they saw him as an amateur, dabbling in something they considered quite serious. But as he circled the ring, he discovered that the others had been watching Harry as much as they had been watching him, and that they observed something in the bird they had not expected. They also paid deference to Chiang. If the white man had the Chinese as an adviser, the white man could well win. Collins heard snatches of talk about Harry's movement and his aggressive disregard for the other men and their foolish birds, how Harry's clucking sounded guarded and considered, even angry. For his part, Collins walked about in silence, absorbing Chiang's insistent instruction.

A crowd of several hundred Ibans circled the ring. Wearing his now-filthy straw hat, Collins strode about like an actor attempting a look of cock-sure confidence. But, inside, he worried terribly, imagining Harry chewed up and dead on the blood-strewn ground. He ground his teeth. His nerves were scattered about, so that his eyes flickered from one thing to another. He willed himself to be calm, but unsuccessfully, having to renew the effort every few moments.

Finally he entered the ring with Harry.

—Good luck, Chiang murmured in his left ear. Collins barely heard him.

He walked to the center of the ring, carefully cradling the spurred Harry, to face a large, gold-colored bird who had obviously already been in a few fights. Its wattle was nicked and scarred. There was a spot on its chest where feathers had not grown back over an old wound. As Collins knelt before his opponent, he looked into the crowd for Chiang. The Chinese stood, arms folded, at the edge of the ring. His eyes gazed steadily at Harry, with the intent passion of a good coach. He expected victory ... hard won, maybe, but a sound effort, something on which to build a chicken's career. Collins glanced at his opponent. He was an old Iban whose tattoos had faded almost completely. His hands looked like pieces of weathered bark. He seemed unable to return Collins's gaze, except for the moment just before the fight when he offered the tuan a weak, acquiescent shrug.

There was no contest. Harry took the bird out in seconds. In a flash of gold and yellow, the other chicken ran away.

There was not even time for the crowd to get into the fight. Harry was victorious so quickly that it was over before anyone could shout encouragement. Chasing after Harry, Collins finally took him up into his arms, and turned back toward Chiang. Chiang remained standing, his arms still folded, as he he looked on with shocked wonder. Collins approached him, very happy. But, for a moment at least, Chiang could not speak. He sputtered a congratulations, but it sounded forced, as though the words had to push their way past Chiang's incredulous surprise.

Harry fought again an hour later, this time against a slow-moving heavyweight, a stupid bird that appeared only listlessly involved in the contest. He was definitely over the hill, and Harry dispatched him with a single, terrible cut to the throat. The bird did not run away, but it became obvious to Harry right away that he had won—spectacularly—so he simply walked to the edge of the ring, where he pecked at a few grains of rice that had fallen from a spectator's lunch.

When Collins took Harry up in his arms and began removing the spurs, he looked the bird over for any wounds. There was not a feather out of place. The bird shivered from excitement. His head snapped back and forth.

Money passed through the crowd in a rapid exchange of bills and jibes and jubilation. Harry caused great wonder. He was a champion, a new champion, everyone said. Collins had to protect the bird against the sudden storm of interest in him. He was finally able to tether Harry, and he wrapped the spurs in some cloth, then put them in his shorts pocket.

He looked about for Chiang, but the Chinese had disappeared. Standing up so that he could see over the heads of the clamoring crowd, Collins saw Chiang walking away, toward the river. There was little sense of triumph in the way he walked. In fact, he appeared to head up the trail as though he had been told of a death or a terrible omen of some sort.

That night, Collins was feted at dinner. The congratulations were universal, and he found himself seated right next to Bawang and two headmen from other houses. One of the headmen actually asked Collins's advice, about a different way he had tried to sharpen spurs for his own bird.

—I'm asking the tuan here because the next tournament's in just a couple of weeks, the headman said to all the others, —and I want my rooster to be ready because, may the spirits help me, he may have to go up against Harry.

Collins was very flattered, though embarrassed by knowing so little. He knew he was the simple beneficiary of Chiang's expertise.

Chiang looked on, and, in response to Collins's inquiring glance, he simply shrugged his shoulders.

—I don't know how to sharpen spurs, Chiang said. The tone in his voice—as though he were hurt or had been shunted aside in some way, unjustly—dampened Collins's enjoyment of the moment. He had wanted to acknowledge Chiang's influence in all this. But Chiang sounded insulted, as though he were being ignored.

After all, Chiang knew quite well how to sharpen spurs. He had spent hours showing Collins how to do it.

Over the next weeks, Collins had little luck breaking through Chiang's new reticence. He visited Chiang's room, went out to the *padi* with him, bathed close by in the river. Chiang was civil, but not much more. He acknowledged everything Collins said to him, even advising him about a cut Harry had gotten by accident on one of his feet. But Collins felt that the high regard in which Chiang had held him before was now somehow lost. Collins looked back through conversations, trying to discover something he had said that could have slighted Chiang. He wondered if he had finally worn out his welcome in the house. Perhaps Chiang—perhaps everyone—was getting tired of entertaining the American.

He spoke with Bawang about it, while helping the Iban one afternoon as he fashioned a new longboat from an ironwood trunk. Bawang chiseled wood from the inner trunk, which was about twelve feet long. The ground around the two men was covered with curved shavings and wood chips.

—You shouldn't worry about it, Tuan, Bawang said. —Chiang's just nervous, that's all.

—About me?

Bawang leaned low over the the trunk, scraping more carefully as the chisel approached the deeper surfaces close to the bottom. Sweat dripped from his forehead onto the wood.

—No, it's that bird of yours. Harry.

—But why?

—Because he saw during that tournament that he may have given away a champion.

—Harry?

—That's right. Chiang thinks he might have made a mistake, that's all.

—Should I give him back, then?

Bawang stood up straight, holding the chisel at his side.

—Oh, no. There's no need for that. Besides, Chiang wouldn't take him back, I'm sure. He's proud of you, Tuan. He's happy he could do that for you, giving Harry to you. It's just …

Bawang shook his head, then lowered himself over the trunk once more.

—It's just that he's afraid.

—Of what?

—That his own bird will lose someday.

—But Chiang's birds don't lose, do they?

—No, they don't. Especially the ones he raises in secret.

Bawang brushed some chips aside.

—Out in the woods.

Collins pointed up the bank, toward Chiang's chicken coops.
—You mean, those aren't the only ones he's got.

—Those? They're just backups, Tuan. His real birds, the ones he raises for the big tournaments, are out there.

Bawang pointed with his chisel over his shoulder, across the river. In the late afternoon, the forest was brown-blue. In the dusk sunlight, it appeared dirty, layered with dust. Light fell against the trees, but was unable to pass through them, clogged as they were with creepers and slash.

—So, Harry was just a backup, Collins muttered.

—I'm afraid so. But we all saw what your bird's really like. Especially Chiang. So you can see why he's worried.

Bawang stood up once more, then ran his fingers over the section of the trunk on which he had been working. The wood was marked by signs of the chisel, but it was quite smooth nonetheless.

—In fact, you know, the next tournament's in a week, and a lot of us have been telling him that he's going to get beat.

To Collins's surprise, a warm vapor passed through his heart as he imagined … as he considered the notion, the naive suggestion, the impossibility of Harry victorious over Chiang's finest fighting cock. He leaned over to run his fingers across Bawang's work. He hardly felt the wood. Harry, his feathers bristling with the wish to fight, filled his thoughts. Harry sniping at the monolithic, unbeatable opponent. Harry obsessed with victory.

Collins and Chiang barely spoke for the next week. Early Sunday morning, as the seedings were being determined, everyone knew that Collins's Harry would go up against Chiang's bird. And so it happened. Bawang summoned Harry first, then his opponent ... a bird whose name brought whispers of sympathy from the crowd. The sympathy was for Harry, because he was to face the finest Chiang could offer, a remarkable and bloodthirsty bantam named Nyamok, a feared bird everyone knew well.

Collins had never seen him. Indeed, he had never heard of him.

Holding Harry protectively, Collins waited outside the ring for Bawang. There was the same pre-tournament activity as before. But now Collins sensed that his presence was not as much of an issue as it had been. While Harry and his tuan owner had been a novelty at the previous tournament, they were now simply contenders. So the Ibans treated Collins with wary, silent respect.

Collins asked Bawang to step away from the crowd, and the two men walked up the river trail. Drops of collected mist fell about them from the trees.

—Yes, well, this bird, Bawang said in response to Collins's question, —this Nyamok is quite a bit more than any you've seen. He's best known for a fight he was in about six months ago. It was ... it was a terrible thing to see.

Collins's heart throbbed as the Iban looked down at Harry, who rested quietly in Collins's arms. Bawang appeared mournful, and the drops of mist rattled about them like an indistinct drumroll.

—You see, in that contest, Nyamok carved up his opponent quite literally, Tuan, Bawang said. —Even after it was dead, lying in a pool of its own blood. And Chiang himself was too frightened to pull him away.

—Frightened by what?

—By Nyamok's ferocity. And there was quite a bit of resentment, as you can imagine, on the part of the poor opponent's owner, who had to stand by and watch as Nyamok flailed at his beloved, destroyed cock.

Collins held Harry even more protectively as he heard all this.

—Chiang gave that man one of his backups, too, Bawang said, —just to keep the peace.

Harry himself seemed unconcerned.

There were some preliminary fights, of little interest. Collins remained on the periphery of the crowd, tethering Harry and remaining beside him as he looked everywhere for Chiang. No one had seen the Chinese, and Collins found this quite mysterious. It was very unlike Chiang, since he so enjoyed the banter of the crowd. But he was not to be seen anywhere.

Finally, several minutes before Harry was scheduled to do battle, Chiang emerged from the forest. Collins saw him descending the trail, his face impassive. He was dressed in a long-sleeved white shirt tucked into a pair of long khaki pants. Both had been ironed, so that Chiang appeared quite natty and sophisticated. He even wore shoes, a pair of plastic Red Chinese loafers with no socks. Collins, suddenly feeling scruffy, glanced quickly at his own shorts and shirt. They were ragged beyond repair. Collins felt a flurry of anger toward Chiang, at the ingenuity Chiang displayed in being so well groomed up here in this jungle. The spotless clothing was like a thumbed nose at Collins.

Chiang carried a fighting cock, a bird that, even from a distance, appeared dark and angry, like a charged rain cloud in his arms.

Nyamok was a black bird whose wings were slightly tinged gray at the ends. His oversized topknot was an even deeper black and it rattled when he moved his head about. Nyamok was larger than Harry, and he looked about himself with what Collins perceived as Britannic elegance. Were he human, Collins thought, he would speak little, yet others would remain silent around him. They'd be afraid to say anything for fear they'd incur his displeasure. There was no feather that appeared ungroomed.

Chiang caressed the bird as they approached the ring, murmuring into the side of his head as though he were giving him instructions. But Nyamok disdained him. He looked out into the distance, treating Chiang's advice as an inconvenience.

The betting increased. Indeed, the fight was delayed because, with Nyamok's arrival, there began a surge of side bets with new odds. How many strikes would it take for the black bird to finish off the tuan's challenger? Would the black bird be wounded at all? Then there was argument about Harry, that he was being undersold, that this was a bird that could beat Nyamok. The odds then grew even that Harry himself would do the worse damage.

Bawang, trying to control the crowd, finally called Chiang and Collins into the ring. Swallowing hard and adjusting his straw hat so that it had a look of somewhat soiled swagger, Collins strode across the muddy expanse to the ring. The two men squatted down before each other. Collins recalled the Friday Night Fights on television back home. Sometimes, when fighters were receiving instructions from the referee before the contest, they stared at each other with fearless aplomb. Now he did the same, gazing at Chiang quietly, putting down his own considerable nervousness. Chiang kept his eyes on Nyamok, giving the impression that Collins and his bird were of little ... no, of no importance.

The birds faced each other. The two men lifted them up, the birds' neck feathers shook with anger, and the fight began.

Harry jumped up against Nyamok, his wings battering the other bird. Nyamok jumped away, as though he were afraid. But as Harry attempted to pursue him, the other bird turned about and attacked him. It was a surprising move. He had suckered Harry into a chase, only to bushwhack him in a moment of perceived triumph. Right away, blood pulsed from Harry's underside, and he jumped again, beating himself against the chest of his opponent.

The crowd shouted out, and when Nyamok too was wounded, a portion of his neck laid open by Harry's quick response, the shout turned to a loud groan of pain.

The fight moved so quickly that it was difficult to tell from moment to moment which bird had the upper hand. In a prolonged flurry, the cocks blustered toward the crowd, toward Collins. With a shout, everyone scattered, including Collins. The birds fought furiously among the people, and flew up against the retreating American. Collins felt a quick burning sensation on his arm. Reaching down, he dropped to one knee. The birds struggled away, back into the ring. Collins's hand glistened with blood, and his arm lay open in a neat cut where he had been hit by one of the spurs. He removed his shirt and wrapped it about his arm, stanching the flow.

The birds fell away from each other, each now badly bleeding. But there was no retreat. Gore pulsed from Harry's belly, yet he remained standing, his eyes intent on his opponent. The feathers about Nyamok's throat were gummy with his blood. It was then that Collins noticed Nyamok's second wound, a neat, incapacitating slice at the base of his left wing. The wing appeared broken, hanging. The bird stared at the ground, exhausted. His breathing was very labored, and he seemed unable to move.

Collins looked at Chiang, whose eyes were open wide with shock at the condition of his bird. But as long as the birds continued facing each other, no one moved to end the fight.

Suddenly, Harry flew at Nyamok once more, and it looked as if Chiang's bird would be overwhelmed. Yet Nyamok summoned up a countermove, and the birds joined again in vicious squawking. They were two flurries of color. They battered each other and fell to the ground again.

Nyamok remained exhausted, certainly near death now.

A whisper passed through the crowd that the tuan's bird had won. Chiang himself looked on in disbelief. Collins's heart pumped with excitement, yet he could barely watch Nyamok's fainting descent. He held the shirt tight to the cut in his arm. Nyamok stumbled. Collins's stomach tightened as he imagined himself suffering Nyamok's wounds.

But then Harry himself turned away, and Collins realized that, in the last flurry, Harry had been struck again. A spur had caught him in the head, and an eye hung down from its socket, blood-soaked, as though from an oily thread.

Nyamok stood above a puddle of blood in the dirt. No one moved, and the two birds suffered their wounds in almost complete, horrified silence.

Then, quietly, Harry dropped to the ground, soiled in his own secretions, and died. He lay motionless in the mud, his feathers stained with blood.

Collins stepped toward his bird. But then he paused a moment. Nyamok still lived, though his wounds were obviously mortal. But he lived. He watched Harry, as though his triumph could somehow keep him alive. Still, no one moved.

Nyamok stepped forward. He clucked a moment, but the usually comic sound of it was liquid with the gore that came up his throat. His legs buckled and he dropped to the ground. His head moved about, but now it had none of the spirited quickness of before. He looked to his left, his eyes appearing glazed, sightless. Finally, his head sagged to the ground.

—Pay up! someone shouted, and the crowd broke into confused noise. —Pay up for Nyamok! The great Nyamok! Money passed from hand to hand, together with wagered packets of rice, bottles of *tuak,* and cigarette tobacco. There was shoving and laughter, voices rising all around the ring in a rush of talk about the fight, and the desperate victory that Nyamok had pulled off. He had won while dying. He had won because he had faced his own death and held it off. Even death had had to wait for Nyamok.

The two men approached their birds. The intensity of the fight gave way to a kind of aimless anguish. Collins was quite exhausted. He knelt next to Harry, then saw that Chiang was standing before him.

—Is your arm cut badly?

Collins exposed the wound, a crisp slice of blood already congealing.

—No, I'll be all right.

Chiang laid a hand on Collins's shoulder.

—Your bird fought wonderfully, Tuan. A champion. A true champion.

He took the few steps toward his dead fighting cock. Collins leaned over to take Harry into his hands. The blood-soaked feathers were like a piece of soiled carpet. Blood slicked his hands and upper arms, pouring from the bird like water.

That evening, a grateful Collins received a gift from Bawang and Chiang—it was a charm hung from a jute strap, which the Iban placed around Collins's neck. The charm was a small bird's skull, dried and intricately colored.

—It's the one I shot out there in the forest with you, Bawang said. —You brought me a lot of luck that day.

They were eating the dinner Chiang's wife had prepared for them, a festive meal made up of their two dead birds. She had spiced the chicken and cooked some greens to go along with it. The rice steamed from a large bowl.

Collins took the skull between his fingers as the Ibans sitting about watching applauded.

—After this morning and the cockfight, you see … I saw that I never would have shot this bird if you hadn't been there, Bawang nodded. He turned toward Chiang. —Don't you think so?

Chiang, still saddened by Nyamok's death, nodded nonetheless. He had helped Collins remove the spurs from Harry's body and sharpen them once more.

Collins, touched by the gift, accepted the headman's kind falsehood, and thanked him. He treasured the skull, finding in the care with which Bawang had cured and prepared it the affection the headman had for him.

Many Ibans were having their meals on the longhouse porch, and the talk had been of all the fights that day, particularly

Nyamok's remarkable struggle to stay alive and win his battle. The lantern light formed ruglike patches the length of the porch.

Collins realized that, worried all along about his decision to quit Kuching, he had not truly considered what had been happening here in the forest. During the past several months, his mind had been down there, arguing with Joe Feeney. But all the while Collins's feelings for the Ibans and for Chiang had been softening and turning toward the kindnesses they showed him. They made fun of him. They laughed outright at how clumsy he was in the forest and the size of his feet and the way his beard grew. But they continued to receive him with open, respectful regard. They were as interested in him as he was in them.

He ran an index finger over the bird's beak, which Bawang had dyed red. Love for these people, a possibility the State Department had not mentioned, had eased into his heart. Unaware of it, Collins had gone about his pursuit of the blowgun and his stumbling struggles up the burning hillside. He had trained and lost Harry Truman. And all the while, love had grown in him.

Now, he lay the skull against his chest. The Ibans who had witnessed the gift-giving appeared to realize Collins's new feeling. It was obvious from the silence with which they enjoyed the moment. They felt the same way about him, observing this white man in the tattered shirt, so careful in the way he had cared for his vanquished bird, so respectful of its task, so humorous in his strange insistence every night on listening to the English spoken on the radio, that strange-sounding mumbo jumbo. And now wounded himself, his arm wrapped in a swatch of clean cloth ...

From that evening on, Collins became entirely immersed in what he was learning. He took care with his appearance once more, though it was becoming, to his amusement, an Iban appearance. He was still enormous, and still had a puffed, milky complexion. But he began cutting his hair like Bawang's, so that it was cropped above the eyes and temples, and long in back, almost to his shoulders. It no longer mattered to him whether the clothes he had brought with him were presentable. Indeed, most of his clothes became so tattered that he no longer was able to wear them at all.

After a year, Collins found that he could go for many days without even thinking about Joe Feeney. Yes, Collins had disappeared. And he was happy with that, happier with each passing month, until the night, in the graveyard, deep in the monsoon forest, when he heard the voice of the Englishman.

7

Bawang and Collins re-
mained alone on the porch
late one evening, after the
news broadcasts, smoking and
talking. As the lantern ran
down, Collins saw rays of
moonlight coming through
the rents in the longhouse
wall. They crisscrossed the
slatted bamboo floor. He
stood and walked to one of the
doorways. Outside, the clearing around the house was
illumined, like a photographic
negative, in bright grays and
whites. The full moon shined
through a break in the trees.

—You like the night?
Bawang asked.

—I've never seen it like this,
Collins replied. He raised his
arm to the doorjamb and
leaned his head against it. He
wore no shirt or shoes. He had
worn his last pair of shorts
until the week before, when
he fell over some rocks in the
river and tore them badly.
Bawang had loaned him a
loincloth. Collins's first efforts
to tie the cloth had been a failure, and the Ibans had enjoyed
how it unraveled around his

knees time after time. After an hour or two of continued effort, he got the idea of how to put it on, though he suspected that his loincloth was attached by fortune alone. Collins cursed his failure to bring along any safety pins.

The entire outside porch and the animal compound in the clearing appeared skeletal and colorless. It was almost a wintry landscape, but for the heat.

Bawang stood next to the American. —You should see it from out there, he said.

Collins smiled. —The last thing Lena told me before I came here was to avoid the forest at night.

Bawang peered into the silver jungle. —Good advice. But I'll take you out there if you like.

Collins ran the fingers of one hand across his chest. Glancing once more at the moonlight, he became for a moment paralyzed by a fearfulness that picked at his gut. The moonlight clarified the forest, making each tree and ashen vine jump from the darkness behind. Beyond the clearing, the forest itself was invisible, locked in a blackness so extreme that it had no features at all. It was a noisy blackness, one in which the steady drone of insects was interrupted by the bluster of howling monkeys and the harsh crack of breaking branches caused by orangutans fighting in the trees.

—It's no more dangerous at night than it is during the day, Tuan. Bawang's voice seemed to make a joke of the suggestion. He waited for a reaction from Collins, then spoke again, as though remembering an important fact. —You just can't see as well, that's all.

—But that's quite a bit.

—No. You just have to worry that you don't stumble anywhere.

Collins's heart scurried about. —All right, he said, clapping Bawang's shoulder. —Yes, I'd like to. Let's go.

Bawang, sensing Collins's anxiety, touched his shoulder as well. —You're sure?

—Of course! Collins's voice contained a grainy quickness. He swallowed, and the two men moved toward the doorway at the end of the porch.

The lights from the longhouse disappeared behind the veil of foliage. They walked a mile and a half through the forest. Even more than during the day, the jungle was all around Collins no matter where he was. It opened to provide passage. But it closed immediately behind. So, he occupied a small emptiness in the forest that filled the moment he left it. Just now, the moonlight provided little illumination at all. It remained very bright where it fell, but it fell only in mottles and flecks, deepening the black of the surrounding flora. Bawang had brought along no light, and when Collins asked about that he said there was nothing to worry about.

—If the forest wants to take you, he said, disappearing a moment, then reappearing in a shard of gray, —a light won't help you.

They descended the trail to a bluff above a broad curve in the river. The tree cover parted, allowing moonlight to fall unimpeded onto the water. Collins knew this place, because it was one of the few in the river that could be crossed without a log bridge. Six boulders formed a crooked alpine path to a point halfway across the water. From the last boulder, a jute bridge led up to the far bank. The bridge was high enough for longboats to pass beneath, and the water below it, a wide spot in the river, was calmer than in the main stream.

The first time Collins had attempted a crossing here, he had made it without a hitch, winning the admiration of the Ibans who watched, especially the children. Though they had doubts about Collins's clumsy flights from one boulder to the next, they admired how ready he was to attempt the crossing. As he strode up the jute bridge, his arms held out, the children applauded. Though he failed the next several times, the Ibans enjoyed those attempts even more as, like a windmill, he flailed from the boulders into the water ten feet below, to be swept several yards downstream.

The storms during the previous days had brought the river almost to the summits of the boulders, and the rushing water now shined like lava in the moonlight, swirling past the peaks. The bridge rose up into the black. The two men sat down on the bluff to watch, and there was a long silence. Bawang was rarely reticent, and Collins saw, in the soft glare, that the Iban was watching him.

—I have a question, Tuan, Bawang said —that I hope won't anger you.

Collins shook his head.

—It's just that … many of us have wondered … Bawang lowered his head and drew with a twig in the mud. He was quite obviously embarrassed. —Why are you here? he asked.

Collins had been surveying the passage of water through the light, and the abruptness of the Iban's question, the demand it contained, surprised him.

—I came to see how the people here live, he said.

There was a slouch of resignation in Bawang's shoulders.

—To learn to farm the rice, Collins grumbled. He struggled a moment. —To study the ways …

—But why are you here?

They listened to the water.

—What happened to you downriver?

Collins did not answer.

—I don't believe you came all the way up here for no real reason, Bawang said. He lowered his head and scanned the mud, looking for stones. Taking one up, he threw it down the bluff.

—My people wanted me to leave Borneo, Collins replied, sighing. He, too, tossed a stone toward the river. —And I didn't want to. So I went into hiding.

—But why did they want you to leave?

A series of images moved with brittle speed through Collins's mind. Eddie descending the longhouse steps in his feathers. President Lyndon Johnson noisily fingering the pages of the *National Geographic*, wondering who in sweet Jesus was the asshole in the loincloth.

—It's difficult to explain.

—Had you committed a crime?

Collins did not reply. He lowered his head onto his arms and listened as the sound of the river welled up about him.

—No.

—Betrayed anyone?

Collins swallowed. If I had let them take me out, he thought, I would have betrayed myself.

—No, he replied.

—Then what happened?

—I worked for my government, Collins said. —I had worked in Sarawak for years.

—Of course. We all see how you speak the language.

—But there are rules that our government has, and they thought I had broken some of them. Rules of behavior, that sort of thing.

How could he explain to Bawang the mistrust Joe Feeney had for such things as the jungle and feathers. He was sure, for example, that, while shaking his hand and telling him how nice it was to see him, Feeney would fear Bawang and worry that he was a dark, immoral power, ruinous to the State Department.

—Oh, we have those rules, too, Bawang said. —It wouldn't be right, for instance, for an Iban to kill a hornbill under the wrong circumstances. To just kill him with no respectful thoughts or anything, Bawang shrugged. —That'd be a terrible way to act.

—But our rules were wrong, Collins countered. —So maybe I did break them, but at least I remained true to myself.

—True to yourself? What's that?

—When you decide that yours is the right way, and that the rules are wrong.

—You have to care about the rules, Bawang said.

—Why?

—We couldn't live if we didn't. You don't steal your neighbor's good luck charms, for instance. You perform ceremonies, always the same, so that the spirits will bless your new children. Always.

Bawang's voice rose as he spoke. He pointed across the river, into the black distance.

—Especially when we leave the longhouse to travel, as you did. Then, we make sure we carry our rules with us.

The urgency of Bawang's advice gave it a burr of disapproval.

—You take your protection with you, Tuan.

—You think I made a mistake? Collins asked.

There was no reply.

—I had to do it, Collins continued. —You can't imagine how impossible it was for me to leave Borneo. I hadn't finished what I wanted to do. I hadn't …

—What did you want to do?

Collins's thoughts cluttered his mind. Indeed, what he had *wanted* was something solely for himself. He had sought solitary escape to dampness and mud and flowers. To the blackness of this jungle.

—White men come and go, Bawang continued. —Eventually, they all leave …

Collins glanced once more at him.

—While we stay here in the forest.

Bawang spoke with a brusque tone that was unusual among the Ibans. At least to the tuans, they expressed themselves with constant politeness.

—You wanted to lose yourself here, he said. —That's plain to see. But there's not much here, Tuan. I've seen the airplanes fly over. I've seen those dragonflies.

Collins smiled. Bawang was speaking of helicopters.

—We don't have things like that, Bawang sighed. The tone at the end was of disappointment.

A cold vapor invaded Collins's feelings. It was regret, coming into him in a kind of undisciplined release. He realized that he could not explain himself to Bawang. He had found, up here, what he had wished to find, but to the Iban that was not much at all. Bawang's voice had yearned with the hope to see a dragonfly once more.

—You know about the Iban *bejalai,* don't you, Tuan?

—When the young man travels, to find out about the world.

—That's right. He can go downriver, mix with the people down there, do anything he wants. Bawang stood up and approached the edge of the bluff. He tossed another stone into the river. —But the young man always comes back, you see.

He stood still.

—So he can tell everybody what he found out. Bawang's skin shone with gray light, while the hair hanging about his shoulders gave off no reflection at all. —It helps the people he left behind, he concluded. —Because he may have found ... I don't know. He may even have found the center of things, Tuan. Who knows?

Bawang's broad face, which during the day was marked with wrinkles and the deterioration of time, bore no such imperfections now. The moonlight smoothed his skin. He looked like a boy-warrior, poised at the edge of the cliff.

—And that may be what you've got to do, he said. —Stay here ... for as long as you like, but go back someday to tell people what *you* saw. Bawang turned from the river. —Even though it's just a lot of trees. He stood for a moment surveying the woods all around them. His profile in the darkness was barely noticeable. —Come on, let's cross over, he said, moving toward the path.

—The river? Now? Collins's eyes moved across the surface of the turbulent water which, as it reentered the forest fifty yards down, suddenly vanished.

—The path back is shorter that way, Bawang said.

Reluctantly, Collins followed him toward the bank. As the path descended, the noise became even louder, so that when they

141

reached the riverbank, the water, now almost white, roared all about them.

—Come on. Bawang jumped the few feet to the first boulder, then to the next. Standing quietly a moment, he looked back. He was stationary as the river dashed beneath him. —Tuan! Come on.

Grumbling, Collins leapt to the first boulder and paused a moment. His footing was secure, but there was little room.

Bawang jumped once more, and disappeared.

—Bawang!

The water took him, his legs the last things Collins saw before he went under, like flailing sticks in the darkness. After a moment, his arms rose in an attempt to swim. But he was taken so quickly that his efforts were useless. Collins struggled to keep his own balance. The Iban disappeared in a trough. He reappeared flowing through a violent riffle downstream, and was swept away.

—Bawang! Collins could go nowhere. The sound the river made—a noisy sigh that rose up and filled the black forest—ran on constantly. He felt that if he tried to move to the next boulder, he would slip off into metallic, glaring oblivion. Bawang was gone.

Collins jumped to the next boulder. Driven with panic, he wanted to make his way downriver. He jumped again, and his foot slipped acoss the surface of the boulder. He tumbled into the river.

Water filled his mouth. He choked, pushing himself through the current as it knocked him about. He went under, came up, and rolled once more beneath the surface, sand-grit burning his eyes. Suddenly he was jammed against a tree trunk. He slid along its length, trying to find something to hold on its moss-slimy surface. It flew from his hands, and a wrenching pain sprayed through his shoulder. He rolled again, shouting as he tried to swim toward the bank. The river entered a stand of thick forest, and, swept along, Collins was hurtled into the darkness. He grasped at the water. He was shoved below the surface, the water sounding in his ears like angered laughter. He could not tell which way the surface was until, without warning, he came into a calm at the river's edge, where he floated a moment, trying to catch his breath. The current pulled at him, and he swam for the shore. In the dark, he encountered the exposed roots of a tree coming down into the water. He grabbed at one of them. After a moment, he found he could stand, waist-deep in the water, in the river silt.

There was so little light that he had to make his way along the bank by feeling for things with his hands. He came to a gravel bar, and crawled up onto it. The black river passed him by. He stood and walked along the bar several yards until, in the reflected, gloomy light ahead, he saw a body lying half in the water, half out.

Collins knelt next to Bawang and placed a hand on his back. When the Iban moved his legs, Collins took his hand and turned him over. Water bubbled from Bawang's mouth, and Collins moved him to his side. The Iban muttered, choking, telling Collins to get away. The American attended to him, holding him as he vomited water onto the gravel.

143

Collins reached down to push the hair from Bawang's face. A serrated gash ran across the Iban's forehead. He tried pulling Bawang to his feet, but Bawang grumbled some crazy mutterings, hardly words at all. Collins took him into his arms and staggered beneath the weight until, righting himself, he turned upriver toward the bank and the forest beyond.

He halted. There was nothing before him. Nothing there, a void, empty of light.

He took several more steps, stumbled on the gravel, and righted himself. Bawang's gritty, wet body felt like dead weight. Swearing, Collins ascended into the black.

He walked for several hours, slipping into gullies, feeling his way. He was turned back by creepers slovenly with sodden moss, terrified when he sensed some drop-off before him, and oddly bitter when he found the drop-off nonexistent. Following the river, he found that knowing the way was less intimidating than not knowing it. But only slightly. There were trails, but he could not tell whether he was on one or not. Most of the time, he was simply lost. The foliage enveloped him. Sometimes he stopped, Bawang so heavy in his arms that he had to set him on the ground in order to rest. Collins stood and looked all around him. But he could see nothing. There were no ghostly outlines. When, finally, he saw lights flickering in the trees far away, he thought they were fireflies. He moved toward them and suddenly realized they came from the longhouse which, miraculously, appeared once more in the moonlight. He moved toward it, almost unable to hold Bawang any longer. He stopped beneath the house, at the foot of the notched log. He had to rest several minutes before ascending to the door. His chest and face were scratched, and he discovered that one shoulder was badly bruised. He crawled up the log and entered the porch, where a group of women had just arisen to begin the morning cooking. They were gathered about a lantern.

—Help me. His voice fell away. The words became confused in gargly coughing. —Please. I've got Bawang.

The women stood haunted in the dark. Collins looked down at himself. Mud scored his body. His skin resembled cancerous scales, in dribbles down his chest and legs. He wiped his cheek, then his shoulder, and blood came away on his fingers.

—Please, Collins muttered. He stepped forward, and the women screamed.

Later that morning, Collins helped nurse Bawang, though there was little the American could do. The longhouse women were far more able, especially when it came to quelling Bawang's rages, when he shouted at everyone, incensed at them for crazed, inconsequent reasons. His head was swathed in rags, at first blood-soaked. After several hours, the rags hardened to a clotted goo. The women left them as they were, afraid that removing them would reopen the wound. So Bawang lay in his frenzy, his bandages turning slowly brown-black as he writhed in violent dreams.

Despite their concern for the headman, the Ibans celebrated Collins. That he had saved Bawang's life was an event remarkable enough. But that he had done it in the forest, beset by all sorts of *antu* ghosts, on a full moon night when the worst of evils breathed from the vines and boulders ... on a night like that, Tuan, they said, shaking their heads and unable to finish the sentence. The Ibans had had to attend to Collins as well. His shoulder was painful, and they made a makeshift sling for him from the remnants of one of his shirts. Washing him was difficult because of the open cuts on his feet. They wrapped his feet in rags, but the insects beleaguered Collins, attracted by the smell of his wounds.

After three days, Bawang's fever left him, and he was able to sleep. Collins sat with him, helping the women give him water and the warm Chinese tea that Chiang prepared for him. On the fourth day, he came into the headman's room to find Bawang awake, but groggy. His bandages had been washed, and he lay on a mat, his head resting on a cushion made of woven black cloth. His skin clung so tight to the bones of his face that it appeared painted on them. It was mottled, splotched dark. His eyes, normally quite black, were covered with a wet gray sheen. He recognized Collins and took his hand, holding it for several moments before turning his head away.

The next day, he was able to speak. Chiang had gotten him to eat some food, and as Collins sat down next to the two men, Bawang's eyes moved about Collins's face. The American helped him with his tea.

—You saved me, Tuan?

Collins nodded.

—How did you find the way back?

—I just found it. Followed the river.

—And you didn't see anything?

—No. It was dark.

—But that's when you see things.

After Bawang sipped from his teacup, Collins took up a cloth and wiped his lips. His own cup of tea remained at his feet, a light mist rising from it in a gray shadow.

—See, it's in the dark that you see the spirits, Bawang whispered.

Chiang nodded.

Collins explained to them that he had been too panicked by Bawang's wound to worry about such things. What he had needed to do was to find the longhouse. Phantasms and weird wraiths … they couldn't have mattered. —It was bad enough as it was, Collins said. There had been no warlocks in the forest. No odd apparition lights. He had seen no mists enflamed with blood.

—But still … Bawang said. He sipped once more from the tea. —If you didn't see them, they must have been avoiding you. And if they were doing that, Tuan, if they were doing that … His head moved back and forth, his eyes fixed on the cup Collins held before his lips. —That means you have something none of us has.

Bawang lay back on his cushion. He closed his eyes.

—Something I've never had, he sighed. —Some unique light.

—Nothing happened, Collins interrupted. —I didn't do anything.

—They left you alone, Tuan, Bawang whispered.

—I've never seen such things, Collins said. —You've described these spirits to me. Living stones. Bad things jumping out at you. But I don't know anything about them. He raised his own cup to his lips. —Although, it'd be something to see. To see what it's like.

Bawang cocked his head and stared at the American. His incredulous look worried Collins. He thought he must have said something offensive.

—You mean you've *never* experienced it? Bawang asked.

—No.

—How is that possible, Tuan?

—I don't know. Where I come from, we don't have such things.

Bawang waved a hand. —Everybody has them. It's like saying

you don't have a foot, or that you don't shit. Everyone has meet-
ings with the spirits.

Collins shook his head.

—And you say you'd like to? Bawang asked.

—Yes.

Bawang's voice seemed to fade. —This is a good thing, Tuan.
Brave. The strain of speaking exhausted him. —But you won't
have any protection.

—When?

—When I take you out to the graveyard.

—Oh, I've been there, Collins said. —Remember, you took me
there a few months ago.

—You've never spent the night there.

Collins sipped his tea.

—And if you want to see the spirits, that's how you do it,
Bawang concluded.

—They're not interested in me.

—Maybe so. And that may be a good thing, because some of
them can be difficult. Bawang gathered his strength as he went on
to speak of the ghostly world. His hands floated above his chest,
in slow accompaniment to his descriptions. —Like Girgasi ... oh,
Tuan, a terrible demon ... Girgasi comes out sometimes, with his
dogs.

Chiang shivered, distracting Collins for the moment. Chiang's
eyes grew large, and he turned his head away, as though unwill-
ing to listen.

—Awful dogs, Bawang continued, —with big teeth. Black
teeth, and eyes that will take your breath away. They're like lights,
but lights made of blood that skitter back and forth. Sometimes
the dogs appear blind, and maddened by their blindness. Other
times, they see you, but *just* you. Nothing else. And they've
attacked people in the night. People who've never been seen
again, or who've been found in the forest, their bowels eaten and

vomited out next to their bodies. And their breath … the breath of Girgasi's dogs poisons the air.

Collins began to reconsider.

—And there's the *antu koklir* …

Chiang shook his head. —Bawang, you shouldn't tell him about those. He shuddered, wrapping his arms about his chest.

—They're women, Bawang said. —And they hunt men in the forest.

—Do they laugh at them? Collins asked. —Chase them around?

—Yes.

—That's not so bad.

—True. But once they catch those men, they do very bad things to them.

Collins raised his eyebrows.

—They attack them down here, Tuan. Bawang pointed below his waist. —Because they're the ghosts of women who died in childbirth. And you, … He gestured toward Collins. —You were the cause of it. So they hate you for it.

Collins wanted to ask what such a ghost looked like. But he already imagined it, a fierce, mad woman swathed in white, floating through the forest, her body enveloping the branches of the trees and passing right through them. She had wild, torn hair. Her hands passed across her breasts in agony.

—Is there anything you can do to avoid her? A gift or something you can give her?

—Nothing, Bawang replied. —Well … you could run away, maybe. He allowed a long exhalation. —Maybe.

Collins respected Bawang's worries. Such demons were very real to the Ibans, and he knew that they saw such things in their dreams. But he felt that people who died in the forest at night died merely of the dangers of the jungle. Simple as that. They slipped and fell. Went hurtling down embankments. Bashed their heads. It was threatening out there, after all. And of course their bodies would be sniffed at and eaten by animals. It made complete sense. But as Collins contemplated Chiang's dour fear, his slumped shoulders, and the way he had turned his head away during Bawang's description of the *antus* ... as Collins considered Bawang's discomfort, and the pained frown that seemed so encompassing ... his own reasonableness made less sense to him. Not that he'd lost faith in himself. It was just that his appeal to logic, his certainty that ghosts were simply neuroses with eyes and odd voices, given life by those who suffered from them ... all that sounded so dry, as though from a textbook, not to the point.

Why not just allow them? he asked himself. For a moment, he did not speak, instead imagining a terrifying passage of mist, cold to the lips and eyes where it caressed him, that whispered to him that he would soon pass from this life, and horribly. Why not that? Or a shimmering striped krait awaiting him in the early morning, that nicked his hand as he reached for a black forest orchid. The gray petals fell to the trail, after the serpent's ghastly disappearance, while Collins frothed and seized in the mud.

—Yes, all right, I'll do it, Collins said. —When you're well. Take me out there.

From that moment, the Ibans treated Collins with unusual reserve. He walked up and down the longhouse porch, seeking the funny mockery that was so normal to their conversation. But the teasing of a group of women weaving in the morning sun, for instance, fell to scared whispers when they spotted him coming their way. The respect they conveyed deadened Collins's anticipation of the event. He had secretly looked forward to the night out in the jungle, certain that nothing would come of it. But, around the Ibans, he felt like some sort of saint come forth from the sepulchre. The Ibans muttered. They bowed their heads. Collins spent a good deal of time by himself. The Ibans looked worried, as though this might be the last they would see of him.

So it surprised him when finally the afternoon came and they took him to the graveyard, and there was no ceremony at all. The longhouse elders accompanied him, along with a gang of children whose chatter belittled what should have been a portentous moment. Bawang, taking Collins's arm for support, told the American he was making a kind of *bejalai* of his own. Pushing a hand out toward the sky, he made a joke of the fading afternoon.

—The sunset's an *antu*, you know, he grinned. Bunched thunderheads, very high up and layered, resembled bloodied ice cream. —Its eyes get red. A drunken demon, Tuan.

The Ibans accompanying them laughed, and Collins joined in. But with his laughter, everyone else shut up.

The graveyard occupied an open space among the trees, above a wide draw in the river. There were mounds here and there, with little organization. The space had none of the scrubbed orderliness of the cemeteries Collins knew. It looked like a vacant lot dotted with bits of rubble and dead underbrush. The Ibans had constructed a small hut, a bamboo platform with a makeshift roof made of leaves. Collins would be protected from the rain here, and his candles could remain lit, sheltered from any wind. He laid his shoulder bag, in which he had brought his notebook and a pen, under the roof. He went to the edge of the bluff overlooking the river. The draw narrowed about a quarter mile downriver, where it flowed into a canyon. The forest formed a gray-green corridor over the river itself, a roofed choir of confusing green.

Collins expected a speech. Indeed, he had made one up himself, something about his readiness to meet with the grand spirits of the jungle. But, to his disappointment, no one said much at all. Bawang especially had little to say, as though there were nothing that a speech could accomplish. Reticence and the simple passage of the river marked the moment, causing a dark nervousness to well up in Collins's gut. The Ibans turned back toward the longhouse, leaving him. Their silence was not that of embarrassment. Or even of simple respect for Collins's bravery. He realized as they walked away that, here in their private territory, where each tree and moss-laden boulder had been known by them since birth, they feared for him. He placed his hands on his waist and looked down at his feet. No matter that he felt this was a lark ... they thought he was a goner.

As the daylight failed, the trees acquiesced to the damp gloom. At the last, the forest was an enormous charcoal confusion, a suggestion of force and growth slowly giving way to the darkness. There was noise everywhere that Collins knew would continue through the night. It comforted him as he sat in the shelter, because it meant that he was surrounded by life. His calm lasted only a moment, though, as he recalled what Bawang had said about demons hiding themselves in the din of the night. In fact, Collins thought, maybe they make the noise. Those were not cicadas and orangutans out there. They were the souls of the dead.

It rained heavily through the night, and the sound of the storm calmed him. At first, he watched carefully for anything unusual, even suspecting that the Ibans might try to play a trick on him with a sham ghost of some kind. But as the hours passed there was nothing except the continuing rain and the noise of howling monkeys fighting in the trees upriver. The darkness was actually calming. The sky was soft black, dark with liquid. A kind of light was in it that allowed Collins to see the outlines of the trees. He began to doze, and had to shake himself awake. Even if he were not visited by some sort of devil, he wanted to experience its absence. He wished to pass through a night immersed in the Iban beliefs. Especially, he wanted to know if those beliefs could skew his own, or push them aside. The chances of such an event were almost none, he thought. But if anything at all happened in this graveyard, he wanted to see it. Even harrying, flesh-burnt dogs nuzzling his shelter ... even if *that* were to happen, he wanted to see it.

Past midnight, the rain increased, coming down over Collins's shelter in rough, scouring bursts. By two, it had passed, and the clouds began breaking up. The sky now was a mottle of stars and blockish clouds passing over. Collins dozed again. There was an unusual, lulled quiet. His head nodded against his drawn-up knees. He could not stay awake and, despite his efforts to move, to change his position, to will himself to wakefulness, his eyes closed, he relaxed, and passed into sleep.

But it was not a comforting sleep. Images passed into his mind … dream images, abrupt, sketchlike memories that hurried by. There was Joe Feeney's disapproval, the squared-off jowls of his face. And Collins himself, in Singapore, receiving his award for excellence of service. His responsibilities … indeed, the actual word, *responsibility*, came into his sleep over and over. But it had an angry tone of an inquisitor. There was the memory of the Belaga rapids, his searches of the radio dial, his explorations, with Bawang and Chiang, of the close, damp woods. All those things showed him walking away, though, from his previous self-assurances that he was doing the right kind of work out here in Asia, the kind of duty that made the U.S. appear as it should, the arbiter of freedom … Jesus, what a cliché! Collins groused in his dream. The provider to those in need, he mumbled, the moral keeper of democratic ideals. No, instead there was Collins cleaning fish. There was Collins playing in the river with children. Poor Harry Truman. And long discussions about rain.

He was besieged by recollection that was, at best, accusatory. Nothing like this had happened to him since his arrival at Nadai, overwhelmed as he had been by the sweat-damp detail that flooded him everywhere he went in the forest. But now he feared that he was using Bawang, Chiang, and all these people just to help himself escape, and that downriver, in Kuching, in San Francisco, in Washington, his own responsibility awaited him.

Nadai was the dream. Washington was the truth.

Then, in his dream, a group of Ibans surrounded him. They

stared at him in silence, asking the same question Bawang had asked. *Why are you here?* But the question so angered him that he took his *parang* from the sheath and menaced them with it. Suddenly he attacked Bawang, and the headman screamed, falling away. But he survived, and grabbed his own *parang* to come after Collins. Collins realized that he had wanted the Iban to retaliate. To punish him. He was defenseless against Bawang's skill. Bawang, his eyes watery with tears, plunged the knife into the American's neck, twisted it about, crushing the bone and nerves, and took Collins's head away. His body fell in a clatter to the slatted bamboo floor.

He saw himself semi-lit by lantern light, brown and yellow. Shadows rippled across him. His feet, covered with mud and deep cracks, lay far apart. The legs were marred by bruises where he had stumbled against roots and underbrush in the forest. The loincloth he wore was badly soiled and, to Collins's terrified amusement, still ill-tied. Collins's chest remained motionless and bloodied, and a swatch of blood covered the bird's-head skull where it lay on the floor. His neck was exploded in a gore-strewn mess of skin and muscle. His head—its eyes, what they had seen—had been tossed away.

153

He jolted awake in terror. Before him, there was a flurry of lights, thousands of them coming from the trees. They rose from the forest floor and swirled over the river. He brushed the sleep from his eyes. His chest quivered as he gripped his shoulder bag with both hands. The lights formed a cloud that moved up and down the river and slowly enveloped the graveyard.

—Fireflies, Collins muttered. A few of them flew into the shelter. They had risen up after the rain, whole swarms of them. Collins put the shoulder bag aside, shaking his head. He wiped his eyes with his fingers and looked out into the graveyard once more.

Like torches in the middle of a swirling chaos, lanterns moved slowly up the river. They cast light on the water in rough circles.

From time to time they seemed to pause, as though the leaden progress they made was yet too fast, too electric. The movement of the fireflies was like frivolity. But the lanterns gave off a kind of shining gloom.

He heard a humming noise coming up from the river in clumps of ragged sound. The lanterns moved closer to the shore and, as they progressed toward him, they held to it, passing beneath the trees, in and out of the darkness.

Collins pulled his knees up and crossed his arms before him, his fingers kneading his upper arms. He could hear his own breath, certain it could be heard everywhere over the sound of the river and the other sounds ... the animals, the numbing blur of bugs and crickets singing everywhere.

And the muscular lurch of the noise coming up from the lanterns as well. Quickly, Collins stood up and jumped from the shelter to the ground. He stepped toward the river. The vision from which he had been suffering, of himself in confrontation with the horrors of Bawang's dreams, passed quickly away. He leaned against one of the trees. The sound in the river was of motors. He leaned forward to listen. Outboard engines struggling against the current.

Jesus, it must be the Americans! Collins thought. They've come to get me.

The lanterns approached the shore below him, and in the noise from the rushing river, in the chaotic din, he heard a voice.

—Put in here, it said.

That's not an American, Collins thought. It's an Englishman!

—In here, you bloody idiot.

8

—Do you fancy putting it out there? the Englishman asked.

Collins motioned to Chiang to keep his mouth shut. He had brought Chiang back out to the graveyard the following morning, to explain to him privately what he had seen. He had no explanation for the Englishman's arrival, with four boats and a dozen Chinese, in the middle of the night this far up in the jungle. But he had to tell someone about it, and he figured Chiang would be able to observe what was happening and keep his mouth shut, at least for a while. He did not want the immediate festival, with *tuak* and wild pig, rice and dancing that the Ibans would surely put on for this Brit, before he had a chance to see who the man was.

But when they arrived at the graveyard, they saw the Englishman, armed with a shotgun, walking up a trail into the hills. He was accompanied by one of the Chinese, also armed, and a Sikh whose gray turban appeared like a smoothly turned bowl on his head. It was a suggestion of neatness that, disappearing up the trail, was an invasion of the forest's general confusion. They had left the boats moored at the bank under guard. Collins and Chiang followed another path in the same direction, Collins explaining nothing to his mystified companion.

—I didn't see a thing! he had said to the Ibans that morning. The recollection of the boats being moored in the morning darkness, and his wonder at why these people had come up the river during the night, a time when normally nobody would travel through the forest ... he had hidden all that in a story about how he had slept through everything. —There was rain. Some animals here and there. The sun came up. But otherwise, nothing.

—Nothing, Bawang muttered. He looked about the group of men gathered on the longhouse porch. The mumbled disbelief that greeted Collins's declaration increased as it became evident that the American had little else to say.

—No, I can tell, Tuan, Bawang said finally. —Maybe they didn't show themselves to you. But you've changed. You're guarding yourself, somehow. Maybe they came to you and you didn't realize it.

—Nothing happened.

—That's what you say. But I think they were there.

Now, Collins tried looking through the trees in the direction of the voice he and Chiang had heard. But the jungle hid everything.

—It's flat enough, isn't it? the voice said.

Collins and Chiang were crouched beneath an ironwood tree at the edge of a small valley about four miles from Rumah Nadai. The valley was separated from the longhouse and the river by a ridge of hills. Chiang had been happy to join Collins because he had wanted to show him the progress of his rice *padi* anyway, a new field he had planted in this valley a month before. Collins had used the pretext of seeing the *padi* to get Chiang away from the longhouse on his own.

The valley was surrounded by heavy forest but was clear enough at one end to be planted. Because it was on flat ground, the rice could be easily cultivated, a much simpler project than was usually the case when the rice was planted on hillsides. As Collins had discovered, everything was done by hand in rough country. He had never worked so hard just to eat. Even getting to the fields could be a trial, since the rice depleted the earth so badly after one planting that it could not be used again for several years. So the longhouse people often had to go far afield for new plantings. Clearing the place, burning the slash, and planting the rice was bad enough. To have to walk several hours just to get there made the farming a sweat-ridden punishment. Having Chiang's *padi* in the forest clearing was therefore a relief. This planting season would be easier than most.

Collins raised his finger to his lips and turned his head to listen more carefully.

—The plane could circle over those hills, the Englishman said. He spoke quickly in a Liverpool accent, like that of the British soldiers in Kuching. —Drop in up there, see, at the long end of the valley, and taxi to a stop right here. I think, I think …

Collins leaned forward. The voice was about thirty yards away, and he lost several phrases as a breeze moved through the forest. He glanced at Chiang, whose eyes were opened wide with anticipation.

—What does he say, Tuan? Chiang whispered.

Collins shook his head.

—Yeh, the wind blows up the valley from the river, doesn't it? So a small plane could land and take off quite easily in that direction.

—Come on, Collins whispered, and he led Chiang toward the clearing. After a moment, they stopped behind some thick underbrush, from which they had a view of the clearing just below. The three men circuited Chiang's freshly planted *padi*.

—Of course, there are Ibans out here, the Englishman said, pointing at the rice plot.

His Chinese companion was dressed in long black pants, a wrinkled white shirt and sandals. The Sikh, similarly dressed, proceeded with his hands clasped behind his back. His headcloth was dark gray and carefully wrapped. He was thin, rather delicate in the distaste he showed for the mud through which he walked, and had a black beard and mustache spotted with gray. The Englishman himself had none of the Sikh's elegance. His thick face was red-cheeked, the result, Collin's guessed, of a life in the wet tropics and too much whiskey. His hair was ginger-red, graying white at the temples, curling from his head like weeds in unruly growth. As he pointed toward the river, the short sleeve of his shirt fell away, and Collins spotted a tattoo of the Union Jack.

—There're many houses on this part of the river, the Englishman continued. —Starting a mile or two above where we moored the boats. But I think we can contain them. Besides, I understand some of them may even be friendly.

Chiang poked Collins's shoulder from behind. —Are they friendly, Tuan?

—I'll tell you in a minute.

—Then, once we get the airstrip in hand and get some equipment in here, the Englishman went on, —we can turn our attention to the road, can't we?

The road! Collins thought.

—Jolly good, the Sikh replied.

The Englishman looked up to the end of the valley once more. A gray cloud settled between the hills. It appeared to be full of water, and it clung to the hillsides as though dying in their arms.

—How long? the Sikh asked.

—A month, the Englishman said. —Two, maybe.

—Excellent. And you're sure you'll be safe?

The Englishman looked into the hills. —Well ... His voice grew thin as the words came out. —Of course, you have to be armed in a place like this.

The men turned on to the trail into the forest, back toward the river.

—Who are they? Chiang whispered to Collins.

—I'm not sure, he said. —They're here to build something. But I don't know what it is.

—Can we find out?

—We have to go down to the river again. To see what they've got in their boats.

Chiang nodded, and he and Collins proceeded across the clearing.

Once again, they followed the intruders cross-country, staying away from the trail. The forest was so thick that, after a mile or so, they lost contact with the Englishman and his companions. But when they arrived at the graveyard, they saw that the boats had been unloaded, and that equipment of some kind was gathered together in canvas tarps that lay piled on the gravel bar along the shore.

After a consultation with the Englishman, the Chinese ordered his men to take up the gear. They lifted the long poles from which the tarps were suspended, shouldered by a man at each end, and awaited the foreman's orders. The neat industry of the caravan seemed pointless in comparison with the forest that rose up all around them. To Collins, hidden behind an ironwood tree hung with chaotically strewn orchids and vines, they were like ants, each carrying a portion of a leaf.

The Sikh climbed into one of the boats. Sitting down in the rear, he reached out to shake the Englishman's hand.

—You'll be careful, then, won't you, Bob? he said.

The Englishman looked over his shoulder at the workers. —Of course we will, he replied. —There's plenty of land out here. He stepped back toward the shore. —And besides, you Sikhs must know that you can't stop the English, he laughed.

The Sikh's smile was marred by a noticeable flinch. He waved toward the driver of his boat, who poled it from the shore. The second boat was manned by four armed Chinese. The third and fourth boats were left behind, tied to a tree.

As the boats headed downriver, the Englishman approached the Chinese, a tall, bent man, about thirty years old.

—So, Po Lin, we'll go up right there, he said. —Over the ridge, and set up camp in the valley.

Collins noted that his spoken Malay was quite good, though heavily accented, like Collins's own. —We should be at work by tomorrow.

When Collins and Chiang got back to the longhouse, they sent several boys out into the forest to call in the people. Bawang arrived after nightfall. He dropped the load of chopped wood that he had carried down the trail, entered his room and laid his *parang* in a corner with his other tools, then went immediately onto the inner porch to join the others. The entire longhouse had assembled, and Collins sensed a kind of traumatized panic in the gathering. Chiang had already described the scene to many, and Collins had to calm him down and correct his exaggerations of the quantity of arms, the militance of the Chinese, and the ferocity of the Englishman's voice as he gave orders.

—What do you think it means, Tuan? Bawang asked. —Why are they here?

—I don't know, Collins replied. —We have to see what they do and, I think, to talk with them.

Bawang nodded with open relief. —Yes, you can do that for us, he said.

Collins stared distantly at his fingertips.

—A white man can talk to a white man, Bawang went on. He looked about the crowd gathered before him, not noticing Collins's scattered glance at the floor.

—Bawang, the American muttered.

The Iban's fresh enthusiasm had brightened his eyes, as though there had never been as clear a solution to a problem as this one.

—You have to speak with them, Collins continued.

Silence fell over the Ibans.

—I can't talk to the Englishman, Collins said.

The faces of the Ibans were like ornaments hanging from a tree.

—Why not?

—You see, it's ... Collins fingered the tattered collar of his shirt, the only article of clothing he had brought with him that was still wearable. He had tucked it in to the loincloth. —I can't reveal myself to this man.

—Why? Will he think *you're* a ghost?

—No, of course not. But he'll see that I'm not an Iban ...

—If he only heard you speak, Tuan, he'd think you were born just a mile upriver.

Bawang held out his arm next to Collins's. The blue tattoos darkened his skin so that it looked like a remnant of tapestry. —Of course, if he saw you, he wouldn't say that you were brown and wrinkled, like me.

—It's just that if I show myself to him, he'll know I'm an American, and he'll notify the people in Kuching that I'm up here.

—So? Wouldn't you like to see your friends?

—They'll make me leave.

Bawang considered Collins's objections, then shook his head. —I don't see the problem. The government wouldn't force a tuan to leave here. The government loves the tuans.

—Oh, from time to time there are bad white people, Bawang.

—Not you!

—Of course not. But the bad ones will come and get me.

Bawang's eyes lowered as he pursed his lips. —I don't believe that the people you come from would make such a dumb mistake. And the Englishman is your countryman.

—No he isn't.

—He is! You speak the same language. You're like us and those Ibans in Simanggang. We never go there, but they are our people. Bawang turned to the others. —Aren't they? We can talk to them. He held a hand out toward Collins. —And you can talk to this man with his strange workers and weapons and tools. Find out what they want.

—I can't. Collins pressed the fingers of one hand to his lips.

—I can, Chiang interrupted. He wore a shirt and shorts—ragged and blotched, but altogether different from the loincloths that everyone else wore. His hair was cut short.

—You think the tuan can find out what's going on just because he's a tuan, Chiang continued. —But those men out there are Chinese, and I can talk with them.

Bawang nodded.

—I'll ask them what they want, Chiang said.

—When? Bawang asked.

Chiang pushed out his lips. —Tomorrow afternoon, after we fish.

—Shouldn't you go sooner? Collins asked.

—They can't do much in half a day. There's time.

—Chiang, you should go as soon as possible, Collins interjected. —These men, we don't know what they have in mind, and I think we should find that out as soon as we can.

Chiang held a hand up, turning his head away from Collins. —Please. I don't think you know enough about the Chinese to say.

—But ...

—I've been up here for years, Chiang went on. He gestured about the circle of Ibans. —These people, for centuries. What can those men out there do before tomorrow afternoon that could be so important. Tuan, it'll wait.

The following morning, Collins helped Chiang clean the fish they had caught. The blood they washed from the deck of Chiang's boat moiled along the riverbank in a dispersing cloud. Chiang continued to appear unconcerned about the task upcoming, but Collins worried what the appearance of so many people so unexpectedly could mean. He had not mentioned what he had heard about the airstrip and the road, wanting to find out why the Englishman was going to build them. But he could not imagine that such things would lead to nothing. An airstrip, after all, meant airplanes.

—Chiang! Chiang! Bawang descended to the boat from the longhouse. His eyes flicked nervously about as he approached. —They're destroying your rice.

Chiang dropped his knife to the boatdeck. He stood, wiping blood from his hands.

Bawang pointed up the hill, into the woods. —They're clearing it away. All of it.

—That's my *padi*, Chiang said. —How can they ... He moved past Collins toward the bow of the boat. —Bastards! The craft rocked back and forth as Chiang jumped to the shore.

—Wait! Collins called out. With Bawang, he followed Chiang up the trail past the longhouse. —You don't know what they'll do!

Several of the Ibans gathered on the outside porch of the longhouse to watch. Chiang's ascent of the hill behind the house was punctuated by his own excited commentary in Cantonese. Collins understood none of it, though its tone was hectoring and outraged. Chiang tramped up the hill. His feet slipped side to side from his flip-flops. He inveighed against his misfortune, his hands waving in the air.

Collins followed him into the woods. The mist made the forest darken and take on a blue tinge, as though all of its individual parts were swollen with water. Chiang got to the top of the ridge and set out toward the Chinese camp. Collins walked swiftly behind him, not certain what he should do. He feared the confrontation and knew he would not be able to intervene. If he stepped in, his cover would be blown. Inevitably Joe Feeney would hear about him—about the weird white man upcountry —and then the State Department would come get him.

But Collins wondered what the Englishman's response to Chiang could possibly be. He imagined a shotgun and lots of yelling in the Briton's north-of-England accent, obscenities that only Collins would be able to understand.

Suddenly Chiang turned and faced him. —Don't come up here! he yelled.

Collins halted.

—These people will listen to me, he said. —They have to. They're Chinese, like me! I don't need you.

Collins looked around. To his surprise, he was alone in the forest, which seemed to hang down about his shoulders.

When he looked back up the hill, he saw that Chiang had dropped down the trail on the other side of the ridge. Above the ridge, the sky—a bank of dark iron—was motionless. Collins returned to the longhouse. The rain that had begun falling increased as he went, finally breaking into an open storm as he approached the house.

Chiang returned two hours later. His shirt and shorts were plastered to his skin. His black hair lay wet about his skull. When he entered the house, he ignored the Ibans. The entire household had awaited his return, worried about what they would do were he not to come back. His wife Ibu greeted him, but he pushed her aside. He swept through the door to his room and slammed it behind him.

Bawang gestured to Collins to follow him to Chiang's room. As they approached the door, they heard the crash of a tin pot against a wall, and shouting. Hurrying through the door, Bawang stopped just inside as Chiang flung himself onto a straw mat and pulled the cork from a bottle of *tuak*. He leaned back and guzzled a mouthful of the rice wine, wiping his mouth with the palm of a hand. He wiped the hand on his wet pants.

—They threw me out! he muttered.

—How? Collins asked.

—There's a foreman there. That Chinese, Tuan. The one we saw at first. And he's Fu-chou.

Chiang shook his head with anger.

—They're animals, the Fu-chou.

He took another drink as Collins and Bawang sat down across from him.

—They don't speak Cantonese. So he tries speaking Mandarin to me. You know what that is, Tuan?

Bawang glanced at both men, mystified.

—Different language from mine, Chiang said to the Iban.

—Chinese speak different languages? Bawang asked.

—Yes! And the fool can't even speak Mandarin. Never went to school.

—What about you? Collins asked.

Chiang's lips puckered with frustration. —I'm not so good either. I listen to it sometimes, you know, on Radio Peking. Late at night. Ibu hates it. It keeps her awake.

—What happened?

Chiang's glaring eyes concentrated on his own foot. —They said that no one owns this land. That the government told them they can do whatever they want with it. They said it was theirs.

—But you do own it. We all own it! Bawang said.

—They just kept working while we argued, cutting down a big ironwood tree with one of those saws, Tuan, the big ones with the motor.

Collins nodded.

—How could we ever cut down trees the way they can, with just our *parangs*. And they looked at me as though I'm a madman. What kind of Chinese would live up here? they said. They told me that they could give me a job, maybe, that I should be helping them out.

Chiang grumbled, intertwining his fingers. —The foreman handed me a shovel and told me to get to work. Told me I'd been living with these Ibans too long. That I'd forgotten I was Chinese. He brought a fist to the floor. —A Fu-chou telling me how to be Chinese!

Chiang took up the bottle of *tuak*, drank some of it, and gave it to Bawang, who held the bottle in his hand a moment. Finally Chiang stood and walked to the rear of his room. Pulling a *parang* from a canvas bag, he moved toward the door.

165

—Where are you going? Bawang looked toward Collins with alarm.

—Back out there. To fight.

He hurried through the door and walked the length of the house, back into the storm.

Bawang headed up the porch himself. Several others joined him, followed by Collins. They all ran from the house, pursuing Chiang as he walked up the trail once more toward the ridge. He was far ahead of them, and eventually disappeared in the forest as he cleared the top of the hill.

The storm pushed the forest about with blasts of watery confusion. As he descended the ridge toward the clearing, Collins wiped his hair from his eyes. The trees undulated overhead—violent, graceful, yet unable to escape the earth that held them. The undergrowth was battered as well by rain. The sleeve of Collins's shirt caught on a snag, and it suddenly ripped. So deteriorated by the weather and sweat that had inundated it over the months, it simply fell from Collins's shoulder. He pulled it off entirely, threw it to the side of the trail, and continued on.

From a viewpoint on the trail, he looked down on the clearing. It was still just a large open space at the end of the valley, but now there were several makeshift huts and a single tent. The near edge of the clearing was covered with slash. Several men working a chain saw were gathered about an ironwood tree, which was a hundred feet tall. Noise from the saw's gas motor rose and fell as the men struggled with it. The tree shuddered, very slowly began to lean, then fell into the forest up the hill. The workers dropped the saw to the ground and took up *parangs* to begin trimming the branches. They climbed up onto the trunk and scurried its length.

Collins wiped rainwater from his face. His wish to help Chiang was sharpened by new, dispirited anger. He could see that Chiang's rice plot had disappeared altogether.

—Look, Tuan, Bawang whispered.

Work on the tree had suddenly halted. There were shouts, and several of the men jumped down to the ground to survey the undergrowth.

Po Lin ran back across the clearing, shouting in Malay for the Englishman. A worker pulled an arm up from the undergrowth, the arm of someone caught beneath the tree. There was furious digging, more shouts. The Englishman hurried across the clearing toward the workers, who finally were able to free the victim and pull him, bleeding badly from the head, into the clearing itself. One of his legs appeared broken, dragged along the ground at an odd angle below the knee.

It was Chiang.

—Come on! Bawang shouted. He and the others hurried down the path. Collins followed, but stopped well before the clearing. When the Ibans surged into the clearing itself, the Chinese workers turned about, alarmed. They hurried to their *parangs,* which they had dropped here and there in the confusion of freeing Chiang from the felled tree.

—What happened? the Englishman shouted in Malay, for the moment ignoring the Iban gathering at the edge of the clearing. He was a chunky man with spindly legs that emerged from his shorts like sticks. He knelt next to Chiang and examined his wounds, then leaned over and put an ear to Chiang's chest.

—Christ, he muttered, quickly taking up Chiang's wrist and feeling for his pulse. —Christ in bloody heaven. He stood and turned around, rubbing his forehead with the fingers of one hand.

The Ibans remained at the edge of the clearing, twenty yards from Chiang and the others. Collins looked on from the forest. When the Englishman saw the Ibans, he gestured to them. There was a kind of solace in the movement of his hand.

—Come on, then, he said in English. The utterance was despondent. —Take him away.

The Ibans did nothing. They were intimidated by the Chinese workers, who had gathered behind the Englishman, holding their *parangs* at their sides. One of the Chinese carried a shotgun.

Then, in Malay, the Englishman spoke once more. —This man's dead, he said. —You can take him.

Collins groaned, and his voice lowered to a whispered profanity.

Bawang approached the Englishman, telling the others from Rumah Nadai to remain where they were. He stopped at Chiang's body and knelt down. His *parang* remained in its sheath as he lay his head over Chiang's heart. Bawang's black hair tumbled across Chiang's shoulder. Chiang stared at the tree cover above, his mouth open, as though to accept the rain that fell across him. An arm lay on the ground, splotched with brown mud. After a moment, Bawang sagged over the body, his hand resting on Chiang's chest.

A moan came from the Iban, low and watery, a surge of helplessness. The fingers of his hand twitched against Chiang's skin. Finally, Bawang stood and looked into the forest for Collins, who remained hidden on the trail. Rain blew across the clearing. As Bawang searched the woods, Collins knew that he wanted some kind of intervention. But he imagined the Americans arriving in boats after he had been identified by the Englishman, taking him away, and throwing him on the plane for the flight to Kuala Lumpur. Then, after a week of psychiatric consultation and general disapproval, there would be a second flight, to Washington, D.C. The vision made it impossible for Collins to move.

But his heart felt shredded, torn up by cowardice.

Bawang shielded his eyes against the rain as he continued peering into the trees. Still, Collins did nothing, even as the fact of Chiang's friendship came back to him. He thought with sorrow of the sense he had given Collins that there was a kinship between them, two odd men trying to make a go of it in this place among these dream-laden, loving people.

Collins felt that his particular cowardice could make no sense to the Ibans ... a tuan who had withstood the worst rigors of the spirit world, who had so stood his ground in the night that no ghost at all had been brave enough to brave him. Yet now he sheltered himself in the woods, afraid to come out. It was the worst cowardice ... faint-heartedness in a valorous man. He felt Bawang's eyes directly upon him, though surely Bawang could not see him. It did not matter. Collins knew that, in this moment, he was betraying Chiang's and Bawang's friendship.

With an imprisoned sigh, Collins's heart struggled to get out, to thrust itself against the memory he had of his obligation to Joseph Feeney. Collins took a step down the path. Right now, he thought, the bastard's looking out into the forest with his bland, punishing eye, searching me out.

He walked into the clearing.

His feet sank into the mud, pushing it aside like black ink, while stones and small twigs scraped his skin. The air had a tepid closeness, and the water that coursed down Collins's body gave no relief at all. Indeed, the water felt like mud itself. His hair fell about his shoulders and remained glued to them as he walked across the field. The Chinese whispered to each other as Collins approached. They were, quite suddenly, jumpy with nervous alarm, fearful of an attack. They observed Collins as though he were a gray phantasm floating across the mud, some fearful vision utterly unexpected.

The Englishman had been trying to cleanse his hands of Chiang's blood. But he ceased wiping them as Collins strode across the clearing. His eyes became pool-like, black stones filled with astonishment. He surveyed the American's white skin, the bird's-head charm,

9

the *parang* sheath and cloth bag swinging from the side of his loincloth, the loincloth itself.

Collins knelt next to Chiang's body and took his hand. There was the illusion of breathing. Chiang's blood flowed from his wounds, pushed from them by a heartbeat. The open eyes appeared to see. But it was all false hope, Collins realized. The blood did not pulse. Rather it oozed ... the residue of Chiang's life now simply dripping from his body to the mud below.

—This *is* a spot of bother, isn't it? the Englishman said.

Collins ignored him.

—Who the hell are you, anyway?

Still holding Chiang's hand, Collins looked up at the Englishman, prepared to see a snide grimace to match the questions. Instead, the man's eyes were bright with loss. He stood to the side, his hands soiled with Chiang's blood.

—He's gone, the Englishman said. —Terrible. But I assure you it was no fault of these men here. He nodded toward the Chinese.

—That's not what they think, Collins replied, looking toward the Ibans. He leaned over Chiang, as Bawang had. But there was no movement.

—Jesus! You're a Yank?

Chiang's fingers came together between those of Collins like dirt-stained twigs. When Collins squeezed them, there was no reaction. The immobility of death seemed to halt Collins's heart, as well. He lowered his head, and rain fell from his hair across Chiang's face. Apologizing, Collins put out a hand to wipe it away. A slow-gathering flow of sorrow inundated him. Sorrow for the death of Chiang. Sorrow for himself and the Ibans. And sorrow for his mistaken notion that up here, in this jungle, nobody would ever find him.

—Right, Collins sighed. —I'm a Yank.

—This is awful.

Collins did not reply.

—But I wonder ... The Englishman placed a hand at the back

of his own neck. —Jesus. He stared at the rain-soaked ground. —Who are you, anyway? Can you help me apologize to these people?

Collins looked up at him with surprise. He felt the man's words—and the vulnerability they expressed—as an intrusion.

—You've got to do that yourself, he said.

Collins motioned to the Ibans to take up Chiang's body. He placed the dead man's hands over his chest, then moved aside as the others lifted him up and began moving from the field.

—But we didn't mean it, the Englishman said. —Don't you see, it was an accident.

They carried Chiang to the trail and into the forest, while the Englishman stood watching. Collins, looking back, actually felt a kind of sympathy for him. The man remained silent in the rain, the Chinese workers moving about him to pick up their tools. His shirt clung to his skin, puddled here and there, translucent. His brusque questions had not succeeded in hiding his fear and obvious regret. Collins felt his own mourning so strongly that the Englishman's concern consoled him.

That night, Chiang's body was washed and his forehead anointed with turmeric. Bawang took a long wooden pestle and laid it sideways across the entry to the house.

—Keeps the spirits out, you see, he said.

—Does it *do* anything? Collins asked.

—No, nothing. But this piece of wood is like you out there in the graveyard. The demons don't know what it is. They think it's a snake, and they don't like snakes.

The Ibans arranged Chiang's wrapped body on a mat on the long porch, his face exposed to the light of a gas lantern that hung above him. The rest of the night was spent in anguish. The voices of the women filled the house with terror for the passage of Chiang's soul. Their faces glowed with the lantern light reflected from their tears. In the morning, they lay leaf-wrapped packets of cooked rice inside the body wrappings and took him out to the graveyard.

When they arrived there, Collins was relieved to see that the boats had disappeared, moved upriver closer to the work site, he guessed. The somber party of Ibans progressed into the cemetery in silence, passing Collins's nighttime shanty. They put Chiang in the ground. His wife, Ibu, knelt next to the grave and placed her hands on her knees. The exhaustion that showed in her swollen face, and the way her thick hands hid her eyes as she broke into weeping, caused Collins's heart to sink. It ached with a kind of near motionlessness. Bawang stood next to Ibu, the ends of his mouth turned down, tears splotching his face.

Late that night, Bawang and the longhouse elders sat on the porch in the lantern-light gloom. Collins was part of the circle. Despite the continuing rain outside, it was a warm evening, so that as Bawang sharpened the *parang* he had brought from his room, sweat glistened like frost on his forehead and shoulders.

After a half-hour's listening to the mumbled talk back and forth, Collins interrupted to ask Bawang what he and the elders planned to do. Bawang sharpened his knife with silent intent, so silent that Collins wondered whether he would ever reply.

—When they kill one of ours, Tuan, Bawang finally said —we take revenge.

—But Chiang wasn't one of yours. He was one of theirs.

Standing in the lantern light, Bawang appeared like a sculpture smeared with dark oil.

—And they didn't kill him, Collins continued. —It was an accident.

—They killed him, Bawang replied. —And we are going out there to avenge his death.

—How?

The blade shined in the lantern light.

—With heads, Tuan. Their heads.

—You can't do that!

—Chiang was a Chinese, yes, just like those men in the forest, Bawang continued. —But he was our Chinese, and that makes him different from them.

Up to now, Collins had simply accepted a cliché about life in this part of Asia, that no ethnic group had respect of any kind for any of the others. That, for instance, the Ibans felt the Chinese were just a bunch of moneygrubbers. Or that, for the Chinese, the Malays were moony and lazy ... worthless. And everyone figured the Ibans to be unlettered rustics, way too enamored of savagery and the English. But Bawang's grief for Chiang was genuine. He sought solace and pleasure in the vengeance he was planning.

For a moment Collins wondered whether Bawang had not got it right. Those men out in the forest did not deserve even the rude huts in which they slept at night. Out there in that clearing, they seemed poised to despoil the lives of many people. Whatever it was they planned to do, they had already done in Chiang. Removing them would be a simple matter, unobserved, quick, and complete.

Sickened by his vision, Collins cursed himself.

—Bawang. You can't, he repeated.

The lantern light extended only to the men seated about Bawang. Their faces appeared flat, as though they had been drawn on a backdrop. Beyond them, in the darkness of the porch, the others sat listening, women and children, weeping. The rafters above were looped with hanging dust and webs. Farther down the porch, so dimly lit that it could barely be seen, the basket containing Sergeant Nakamura and his friends hung from a ridgepole. It resembled a black smudge.

Bawang's hand remained poised on the blade. —Why not?

—It would be murder, Collins replied.

The others whispered to each other. Collins sensed their disapproval of his remark, and Bawang continued his work. There was no answer.

—Those men out there are just workers, Collins continued. —They don't mean you harm. They're being paid by people in Kuching, by people in ... I don't know, England or somewhere.

—They're the enemy, Bawang said.

Collins was frightened by the murmur of agreement that came from the others seated about the mat. How much can I disagree and still be safe myself?

—You've lived in Sarawak a long time, Tuan, Bawang said.

—Yes.

—But you don't seem to know much about why we take heads.

—Yes, I do …

Collins faltered, dropping his chin toward his chest. Bawang was right. What Collins knew of the practice was contained in the numerous baskets of heads he had seen in longhouses here and there, what he had been told about the past by nostalgic head-men, and what he had read in anthropology books—British anthropology books, as it happened—which described head-hunting in such a plodding way that one would think the practice had no blood in it at all. No thrill. No pleasure.

—The white men I told you about, during the war? Bawang said. —They were like you. They were angry with us when we took the Japanese heads. We never learned why.

Bawang laid the *parang* on the mat and wiped his fingers on a dirty rag.

—But their companions, he continued, —those strange mountain men … they understood. They appreciated what we did.

—And what happened?

—The white men were angry with them, too! Bawang laughed, looking around the group for agreement. —But it was they who showed us how to get into the Japanese camp. And it was they who told us we should take only *some* of the heads, not all. Do you know why, Tuan?

Collins shook his head.

—To horrify the Japanese! What kind of people must we be if we sneak into their camp in the middle of the night, take a few heads in complete silence, and let the others wake up in the morning to find what has happened?

Bawang reached to his left and patted the straw mat.

—The man sleeping next to you, maybe, your good friend. Lying on his mat, the body the same as always—on his back, his arm across his chest, sleeping—all the same, except, except ...

Bawang drew an imaginary line across his throat, then pretended to pull his own head away.

Collins grimaced. —So ...

—Tonight, Bawang interrupted.

—Christ in heaven, Collins said, his sudden change to English startling the Iban.

—What was that, Tuan?

—Nothing. Nothing. Collins gripped his hands before him. The nails were badly abraded. The hands themselves were thick, like a workman's, without nuance.

—You want to come with us? Bawang had ceased sharpening the *parang* and, standing up, slipped it into its wooden sheath. The dark ironwood was intricately carved and decorated everywhere with the feathers of hornbills. The white and black plumes provided a glimmer of delicacy in the dampness of the longhouse porch.

—No.

—I didn't think so. The Iban's remark was filled with disdain. He secured the *parang* in the sheath with a piece of rattan. His bowed legs darkened in the low lantern light. He caressed the sheath and its feathers, making sure they were properly positioned down his leg.

The other Iban men stood up as well. Each had a *parang*, but of the more workmanlike sort they used in the forest. Only Bawang's was artful. A knife like this drawn from such a sheath would glorify the killing. Maybe the headman's the only person in the house qualified to decapitate someone with grace, Collins thought.

—Don't come out in the jungle, Bawang said.

—I …

—It'll be dangerous out there. It would be terrible for us if we lost you.

Waving a hand to the others, Bawang motioned toward the door at the far end of the house. With the women and children, Collins accompanied the men, and watched them negotiate the notched log leading to the ground. They carried no lights. They gathered at the bottom of the log.

—We'll go up there along the upriver path and come in behind them, Bawang said.

It was a roundabout route that would take at least an hour and a half.

—That way, they won't be prepared for us.

Turning away, Bawang led the men toward the river. There was little to see. In the distance, the trail disappeared into simple black. But the noises from the forest were unmistakable, and the rustle of orangutans hurtling through the trees barely hid the tortured sighs of the birds and the monotone cicadas singing in the downpour.

Collins returned to Bawang's room. He knew he would have a moment alone there. The Ibans respected his privacy when he was in the room by himself, which was usually when he was preparing for bed. They seemed to think that the white man's toilet was an exotic procedure, not to be witnessed. He pulled out his shoulder bag, scattered the contents on the floor, and searched through them for a penlight he had brought with him. He walked to the kitchen at the rear of the room.

His heart tightened, and he paused a moment, staring at the light in his hand. It was so small that he wondered how it could possibly show the way through the forest. It was the only object in his possession left over from his life in the United States, and he turned it on, to make sure it worked. It cast a strong, but quite limited, beam across a few floorboards.

Collins rubbed his forehead with one hand, paralyzed by the choice before him. The Ibans would throw him out if he interfered. Surely. Maybe they'd kill him. But the Englishman was sitting out there in his tent, a victim awaiting an undeserved execution. Even so, Collins was so angry with the Englishman that he considered putting the light back in his bag and simply going out onto the porch again. The Brit and his project, whatever it was, were so goddamned thoughtless. He was the enemy. Though if you warn him, Collins thought, they'll open fire on the Ibans. So, sure, maybe you'll save his life. But many others will die. People you love. And the Englishman will be able to just carry on.

But, he's a compatriot, Collins grumbled to himself.

The anger in his heart overtook him, anger at being compromised by this situation, at having his private escape now so ruined. But Collins could not bear the notion of the man's throat severed in the muddy darkness. Or the bodies of his workmen strewn every which way. He had to warn him, even though the need to do so outraged him.

Looking over his shoulder, to make sure he remained unseen, he switched off the light and walked out the door at the back of the kitchen to a rickety ladder that led to the ground. From the bottom, he looked back at the longhouse. It resembled a weather-scarred, rattan sailing ship, its roof a thatch prow, its porches falling-apart decks. The house actually seemed to list, pushed to the side by the windblown forest.

Collins walked the length of it, frightening the animals sequestered beneath, to the beginning of the ridge trail. He did not use the light at first, worried he would be seen. Moss hanging from the low branches brushed his face. He stumbled over rocks, falling a few times onto the trail. Finally reaching the ridge, Collins decided to chance the light. It cast a semicircle three feet before him. Beyond the circle, the forest was just as black, just as immeasurably huge.

He would arrive at the workers' camp well before Bawang, but he worried how he would get into it. The Chinese were already terrified by the Ibans. With Chiang's death, they would be looking out into the forest, imagining the worst kinds of reprisals. And the worst kind of reprisal was about to take place. Collins would have to reveal himself. But doing that might get him killed. He hurried up the ridge.

He stopped at a high point on the trail. Below, he made out the Englishman's tent, lit from within by lantern light. The workers lived in the four huts nearby. They were platforms made of bamboo slats, on stilts that lifted them up above the insects and snakes crawling about the forest floor. Overhead, each hut was covered by a palm-leafed roof, three feet above the platform. The men slept inside. Their possessions, which were very few, made up their pillows. All of the huts were lit—three of them by lanterns, one by candles set out on a small platform at the entrance. Each hut was guarded by one of the men sitting on the platform with a shotgun, looking out into the rainy darkness.

Collins swore as he imagined standing up and waving his penlight in the air to identify himself. He saw it flung into the underbrush as the Chinese opened up on him, taking him out with their small arms. But, fellows! he imagined himself gargling as he went down in a hail of buckshot. I'm State Department. I'm AID!

He moved along the trail toward the camp, feeling his way through the trees. He walked as silently as possible, but stumbled and slid down the trail several feet. He dragged ferns and underbrush behind him, and water fell everywhere. Collins stood and continued, stopping finally behind the twisted roots of an ironwood tree, about thirty yards from the camp.

Making sure he was protected by the tree itself, he gathered his nerves and took in an exhausted breath.

—Hello, Englishman!

There was immediate gunfire, and smoke everywhere. Buckshot tore off a section of bark well above Collins's head, spraying him with shards of wood. He cowered against the tree. Nervous voices shouted at one another in Chinese. Collins heard one of the workmen castigating the others, yelling at them, he guessed, to hold their fire. His shoulders rattled against the tree, and he looked out.

—I'm alone out here! His voice cracked. Clouds of gray smoke passed before the lanterns. He saw a black figure come out of the tent to peer into the forest.

—I want to talk with you, he shouted.

—That you, Yank?

Collins lay his head in a hand. Who else *could* it be? Peter Pan?
—Will you tell your people not to shoot?

—Have you got a torch of some kind? the Englishman asked.
—So we can see you?

Angrily Collins debated the request, worried he was being set up. But after a moment, he turned on the penlight and waved it in the air.

—Up here! he said.

—Christ, the Englishman muttered. —How'd you get so close?

—Can I come down?

The Englishman discussed with Po Lin what to do. The foreman advised doing nothing, wanting to keep the foreigner out there where he was less of a danger, more in danger himself actually, where he had to contend with the terrors of the jungle at night. The Englishman argued against that. Collins heard two phrases in English among all the heated exchanges in Malay. One of them was —Bloody Yank's got to be on our side, doesn't he? The other was —Bloody idiot's a white man, isn't he?

—Do I come down?

The Englishman ordered the men to hold their fire. —Come on, he shouted to Collins.

Waiting a moment, Collins finally stepped from behind the tree, holding the penlight before him. He worried the batteries would fail. He awaited a barrage of shotgun fire.

He entered the camp. The workers looked out from their shelters, training their shotguns on Collins like phantom sticks. His heart was in chaos. His feet sunk into the mud as he stumbled across the clearing. At last he confronted the Englishman.

—My name's Collins, he muttered, out of breath. —I'm with the Department of State of the United States government.

—That's bloody wonderful. I'm Bob Rooney. The Englishman eyed Collins's loincloth with distaste. He raised his lantern to get a look at Collins's face. —I'm with Lee Fan Lumber, Limited, of Kuching.

—You're Irish?

—Of course not. I'm a British citizen, like everyone else, Rooney said. —And I feel like a fool, I can tell you, being terrified by an idiotic American on a night like this. And in a place like this. But there it is, Yank, and I'd like to know what you're doing out here.

—That's not important, Rooney. What's important is that those Ibans from Nadai are upset about the man who died here the other day.

—They're upset about it! Imagine what my company will think.

Collins grimaced. —They're coming out to get you.

—Out here?

—Yes!

—Not in the middle of the night, Rooney said.

—Now!

Rooney placed his hands in his pockets and turned aside. He shuddered, as though he realized what was about to happen. Nevertheless, he took on an air of defiance, almost jauntily scratching his head.

—What do they plan to do, Yank, take our heads? Rooney laughed. His face appeared cut up by splinters of light.

—That's right, Collins replied.

Rooney's smile fell away. —Listen, it's dangerous enough to be sent up here into this forest like I was. Rooney gestured toward the Chinese. —As these men were. But you appear to have come up here on your own.

—That doesn't matter.

—It does matter. Because if I know who you are, Yank, and why you're here, I'll know better whether I should believe you.

—You've got to get these people out, Collins said. —The Ibans think you murdered Chiang.

—We did not.

—Of course you didn't. But for them the truth is that Chiang came out here to protect his property.

—It's our property!

—It's their property. Has been for hundreds of years.

Rooney waved a hand before him.

—You've got to listen to me, Collins insisted. —Here's what you've got to understand, Rooney. You've got to get your people out of here, get them out, on foot, by boat, it doesn't matter.

—Why? They're just savages, these Ibans.

—Whatever you think they are, they're coming to get you.

Rooney looked out into the jungle. —How do you know this?

—Because I live at Rumah Nadai.

—You!

—I've been there for a year. I've lived in Sarawak for many years.

—And you've allowed them to do this?

—I don't have any say in it.

—You don't! A white man like you, I'd have thought you'd be king by now, Yank. The king of Borneo and all the world.

There was a shotgun blast across the clearing. Collins ducked, throwing an arm up over his head. Panicked shouting, in Chinese, was blotted out by the rain.

—These men are nervous, Rooney muttered. —They don't know what's out there.

—You've got to go, Collins said.

Rooney remained hesitant. —How much time've we got? he said finally.

—Fifteen minutes, Collins replied. —Ten.

Rooney anguished, the fingers of his right hand rubbing his forehead. Collins wondered what kind of man he was. Had he ever been in Sarawak before? Had he fought the Japanese? Did he have a wife?

—All right, Rooney whispered. —You think we should head downriver?

—As fast as you can. All you have to do is go downstream a half hour or so. Wait until sunup, and then continue on. When they get here, and you're gone, they won't know what to expect. They'll think ... Collins shook his head, looking for the words. —They'll think you've run away.

—Up your bum, Yank.

—Don't be insulted, Rooney. Just go, for God's sake.

The Englishman looked out into the darkness again. After a moment, he sighed and moved toward his tent. —Don't know what the chaps in Kuching'll say.

—Tell them you saved your workers' lives.

Rooney pulled aside the tent flap. He moved inside and took a paperback from a metal table, a few pens, and some shirts, all of which he put in a rucksack. He put on a soiled Australian army hat, then came back into the darkness. Collins muttered nonsensically. He figured Bawang was out in the woods with the others, watching.

—But I still don't understand how it is that you're here, Rooney said. —We never expected to find an American out here. He gazed at Collins, hoping for an explanation.

—You must get these men out of this camp, Collins snapped.

Rooney hurried across the clearing to the workers' shelters. After some quick instructions, the men gathered their belongings.

Rooney approached Collins once more. —I guess I should thank you, he said.

—Go on!

Rooney shrugged and, shouldering his bag, turned away. He joined the workmen at the edge of the clearing and, silently, they entered the jungle.

After a moment, Collins looked about the camp. The shelters remained semi-lit and small, glittering fissures in the dark. Rooney's tent flap was open, and Collins went inside to get out of the rain. Rooney had left several things behind. The American, in his perusal of them, dripped water everywhere. There was a notebook, a kind of log Rooney had been keeping. Collins was surprised by how pedestrian the entries were, in pencil, a sentence or two a day about the weather, nothing much. In one corner of the tent, next to his cot, there was a shovel and several boxes of shotgun shells, plus a carton of tinned beef stew. A mosquito net hung about the cot, and, unaccountably, a pair of leather slippers was lined up beneath it.

The tent was made of canvas, and the light that was cast over everything carried the gray-yellow hue of the cloth. There was nothing in the tent to indicate who Rooney was, nothing of a personal sort that would say what his life had been like before he came to Nadai. Collins sat down on the canvas chair next to the small table. He leaned his head on the palm of a hand, and water slid down his arm onto the table. So neither of us knows anything at all about the other, Collins thought.

He turned the pages of the notebook, water from his hair splotching the few observations Rooney had made. —Weather bad today. Too much rain. No contact with the Ibans.

Collins imagined the career Rooney had built. Maybe he was an army man, who had served in Malaya. Loving how he could dirty his hands in the rubber plantations or the tin mines, he had decided to stay on and work in the country that gave him so much life.

—He's like you, maybe, Collins muttered to himself.

Finally Collins came to those pages in Rooney's log on which nothing was written at all.

The rain falling against the walls of the tent diminished, and only the large drops that had accumulated on the trees rattled the dark canvas. After several minutes, there was silence. The insects no longer sang. There were no struggles between the animals in the trees. Beyond the small triangle of light thrown out on the mud by the Coleman lantern, Collins could not see any difference between the jungle, the mud, and the sky. The workers' huts across the clearing looked like rickety craft hanging in the middle of the universe. Their lanterns turned the darkness around them to a soft, confined blue. Otherwise there was no variation on the black. Collins felt that it was like the darkness that would surround him if he were buried in the middle of a mountain.

A shadow—a dark man in a loincloth—stepped up to one of the workers' huts, a silhouetted *parang* raised against the light. He reached for a ragged shirt lying on the straw mat inside and threw it into the darkness. There was a hurried search.

—Where are they? the man yelled. It was Bawang. —They're gone!

Collins lifted a hand to his mouth. Holding his breath did little to quiet his heart. He tried to swallow, but could not. Several Ibans now appeared in the dim light.

They destroyed the huts, knocking over lamps and setting the thatch on fire. It was a battle, but a fruitless one waged against ruined hopes with shouts of anguish and anger. Collins hurried into the darkness in panic, as though the night's black would save him. It had started to rain once more. He stopped in the middle of the cleared field. Water slipped down his body to the ground.

Where are you going to go? he thought to himself. The flames quickly diminished, and steam rose toward the trees. Collins floated in the darkness. He felt that his body had disappeared.

But, he discovered, so had the Ibans. They had left the huts as they burned, and now Collins could not see anyone. The Ibans had vanished, leaving Rooney's tent untouched. There was only the hissing leftovers of the huts. Collins waited for a few minutes, finally convinced that Bawang and his men had returned to the forest. Angered by Rooney's obvious discovery of their plans, they must have given up. What would be the point, anyway? Collins thought. The enemy was routed, scattered into the darkness.

He returned to the tent. The light and the few familiar, tawdry objects reassured him. They made him feel as though, in fact, he had not vanished. He was indeed still Dan Collins, still from San Francisco. He turned toward the tent flap to look out. The ruined huts barely gave off any light at all.

Collins sat down on Rooney's cot. The Englishman had left behind a single shirt and two pairs of shorts, and though they were badly wrinkled, they were clean. Collins, his loincloth sagging down his hip as though it were about to fall off, stood up and took a pair of shorts from its metal hangar. He removed the loincloth. Then, stumbling on one foot, he put on the shorts. He took the shirt from the nail on which it hung and pushed his hands into the sleeves, bringing it up over his shoulders. It was made of cotton check, in black and white. Its collar was frayed. He turned toward the shaving mirror Rooney had left nailed to the center post of the tent.

There were mirrors in the longhouse, but Collins had usually avoided them. He did not want to see how he looked. His clothes had been so quickly ruined that he supposed he had suffered just as much himself in his own way. The clothes had reminded him of his duties and how important it had once been to him to represent the State Department well. But now they were gone. He had feared that his appearance would prove to him his own irresponsibility, and how he had betrayed the work he had done. Now, though, he was alone in the haven of the tent, a haven sprinkled sparsely with civilized objects, like the bar of soap and the dented pewter cup that Rooney had left behind. Collins turned toward the Englishman's mirror.

The beard had no shape. The skin around Collins's eyes was wrinkled even more, so that now there was a shoe-leather look to

it, but of old, unpolished shoes. The eyes themselves were saddened, perhaps dead, he thought. His lips were badly cracked.

Sitting down on the cot, Collins leaned forward and placed his
hands over his face.

Suddenly, there was a crash at the entry to the tent. Collins fell
back against the cot and threw his arms up. Bawang came into the
tent, raising his *parang* above his head. Collins scurried from the
cot to the floor as Bawang lunged at him. The *parang* slammed
into the wood of the cot. Bawang pulled at the knife, struggling
to yank it loose.

Finally he pulled the *parang* free. Collins scurried across the
floor. He screamed, rolling about and covering his head with his
arms. Bawang lunged at him.

—Bawang! No! Please!

The Iban stumbled and fell gainst the tent pole. His eyes
widened with angry surprise. —Tuan, what are you doing?

As Collins lowered his arms, Bawang allowed the *parang* to fall
to his side. He held it there a moment, his hand twitching. 187

—Why are you here?

Collins attempted an answer, but he could not speak. He imagined that the *parang* had a life of its own. Irritated by the brush of
feathers against its side, the knife would be further incensed by
the fact of Collins's being in the tent, rather than the Englishman's. It wanted to strike again. Collins tried to fashion a smile,
but his mouth felt imprisoned.

—I'm sorry, he said, after a moment.

Bawang replaced the knife in its sheath.

—I came out here to tell the Englishman what you were planning to do.

—So it was you.

Collins folded his hands between his legs. Bawang's body was
now so resigned-looking that his heated glance seemed out of
place. He sagged before Collins, his shoulders sloping at an angle.
Water ran from his black hair down his face. A puddle formed at
his feet.

—Yes, Collins replied. —Yes, it was. He dropped his forehead into a hand.

A look of dismayed unrest caused Bawang's lips to tighten. —Tuan, he said. —You are a fool.

Flames burst through one wall of the tent, and suddenly it raced with fire. Bawang hurried into the night, and Collins stumbled toward the entry. He fell over Rooney's slippers, and his shirt caught on fire. Screaming, he crawled from the flames and rolled down the short rise on which the tent stood. The shirt sizzled in the mud. A shout went up, triumphant voices through the rain and smoke. The flames rattled against the darkness. Collins saw the faces of about thirty Ibans, their eyes transfixed by the fire.

Bawang stood before them, yelling at them to keep their guard, that the Chinese could be waiting out in the forest to counterattack. But the Ibans paid no attention. They watched the fire, and Collins, spattered with fresh mud, was struck by their almost wooden immobility. Their *parangs* hung down from their hands. In a moment, the clatter of the fire died away.

Collins's vision of the Ibans crawling into the camp and severing the heads of a few workers, leaving them butchered in their huts like pigs on a grate, had put aside the anger he had felt about the airstrip and the tree cutting and poor Chiang's death. That vision, if allowed to become reality, would have driven him mad. But now, because of his intervention, the Ibans stood about suffering in crestfallen disappointment. The smoldering bits of cloth and thatch rising into the trees, glowing for a moment and then disappearing, were like wisps of a dream, like hopes drying up.

As the fire receded, Bawang stepped onto the smoldering wood floor of the tent. He held a lantern up and surveyed the floor closely, pushing aside Rooney's charred canvas chair. Swirls of smoke gathered about him. Collins sensed that Bawang was searching for some indication of who the Englishman was and what he had been doing here. But the wood gave up nothing, and

Bawang shook his head finally, mumbling to himself. He stepped down from the platform to join the others. The lantern cast an uneven light in a circle about Bawang's feet and those of the other men.

—Bawang, Collins said.

The Ibans turned and faced him. They had evidently not known that it was with Collins that their headman had been struggling in the tent. They too had thought he was the Englishman. Seeing him now, their faces turned glum with surprise.

—The Chinese won't come back, Collins said. —And neither will the Englishman.

He wondered for a moment whether this could possibly be true. Then he recalled the Chinese boatmen down in Belaga, their reluctance to come into the deep forest. The Chinese feared the Ibans, and Collins imagined that none would ever volunteer to come back up here.

—They knew we were coming, Bawang said to the others. —Because Tuan told them.

189

Collins grumbled silently, proud of what he had done. Drops of rain fell through the circle of light like cold needles.

—Shall we kill him? Bawang asked.

The rain splattered against the mud, and Collins's heart raced.

—Because, you know, Chiang is still dead. We've gotten no revenge, and this tuan is all we've got left. We could hang his head in a basket of its own, Bawang concluded.

Collins studied the mud at Bawang's feet, its dampness shimmering in the white glare of the lantern. His mouth was suddenly dry, as though coated with dust.

—No, Bawang said, finally. —He betrayed us, but no. The tent platform now gave off no light, and the lantern in the headman's hand hissed. —The tuan betrayed us. But to kill him, our own guest, would be murder. Shameful. It would be shameful.

A grumble of agreement came from several of the men, and they turned away. Collins remained where he was, penitent, his hands jammed in the pockets of Rooney's shorts. The Ibans began moving across the clearing. One of them stooped to pick up a shotgun the workmen had left behind.

Collins sat down on the platform. He feared the Ibans would come back for him. He was certain of it, since he had angered them so. He waited in the darkness, his heart pulsing like a sharp stone in his chest. Finally the rain ceased altogether, the clouds passed away, and stars appeared. He could see little, though he heard the wind all around him. It came from no particular direction. The stars glared in clouds of silver light. The wind buffeted him through the night, growing in strength until, finally, it simply ground him under.

At first light, Collins headed toward the river. Wisps of smoke continued to rise from one of the workers' huts. Tools were scattered about, and miraculously a lone lantern still worked. Propped up in the mud, its hiss sounded faintly through the silence.

A white fog rose from the valley floor. The lower edges of the trees receded into it, as though they were made of paper. The fog's movement across the clearing obscured the chewed-up waste that had been Chiang's *padi*. The fog gathered about Collins. It was clammy, like grease.

He walked up the trail. After several yards, he looked back over his shoulder and saw a movement from the far side of the clearing. Bawang and a few others walked out into the open.

Collins turned and descended once more into the clearing. In the discomfort of the heat, his heart began to swell inside him and to weigh down his chest. The Ibans stopped in the middle of the clearing, the fog surrounding them up to their waists. The morning light was not yet strong enough to illuminate them entirely, and they stood in silence, silhouetted against the forest beyond. Collins felt there was little he could do to make contact with them. They simply watched him. He remained still, though for the moment he felt—he hoped—that they might still care for him, despite what he had done. He could not bear leaving them.

Finally, Bawang walked toward him. He did not appear angry, though there was a look of disgruntled exhaustion on his face. His eyes were puffy. He still wore the *parang* he had used the night before.

—I'm sorry, Tuan, he said as he stopped before Collins.

The American shrugged. —For what?

—That we didn't explain ... well, that we didn't explain proper manners to you.

The fog settled about both men.

—Anyone who really understood what it means to take a head would see ... Bawang raised his eyes toward Collins's. —Forgive me. Would see how thoughtless it was, what you did last night.

—I apologize.

—I mean, we thought that that white man, and the Chinese he had with them, we thought they had a pact with the spirits!

—No, no. It was me all along. And, you see, I couldn't allow them to be ...

—Wait, Bawang interjected. —Wait. It was our fault.

—Your fault?

—You can't expect much from someone who doesn't know ... well, you know, the rules. So, it wasn't your fault that you warned those men that we were coming.

—It wasn't?

—No. If you'd been born an Iban, you never would have done such a thing.

—I suppose not.

—So we came out here to ask you to come back to the house. Bawang gestured toward the others waiting in the distance. —Poor Chiang would want that. And we want it.

Collins placed his hands on his waist and looked at the ground. The moment he arrives in Kuching, Rooney will call the consulate, Collins thought.

—The Americans will come, he said. —To get me.

—Then we'll have a festival for them. And it'll be interesting, to see what the Americans are like.

191

Collins tightened his lips.

—I suppose they're all like you, Bawang said. —But, in the meantime, come back with us. He placed a hand on Collins's arm. —You're a brave man, Tuan, he said. —You don't understand much. But you're very brave.

The two men moved across the clearing toward the others, who clustered around Collins and greeted him. He felt his shoulders and back being pummeled. The group formed a tight circle around him, and he thought for a moment that they were going to lift him up on their shoulders, like a penitent king returned from an unpopular war. The congratulations lasted for some minutes, until finally the group turned and walked past Chiang's uprooted *padi*, past the ironwood tree that had felled him, and up the trail toward the ridge. Walking back to the house, they reminisced about Chiang and discussed how they would have to replant his *padi* despite the rankling, unfortunate luck that probably filled the valley now. Someone suggested that Collins should take it over, that, with the help he would get from the spirits, it would yield a fine crop. Collins accepted the gift, and said that he would get to it the next day.

Which he did, with the aid of several of the men from the house. He cleared the site again, then planted the shoots in the ground. He built a palm-leaf shanty like those of the others. He weeded. He spent his nights in the longhouse listening to the radio, using the last batteries from Chiang's shop, until they ran out. There never was news about him of any kind at all.

During the following year, the jungle covered over the ruined Chinese camp. Collins sat with Bawang in his shanty on late afternoons, enjoying the rain squalls as they swept the valley. He gathered together what he would tell his American captors, and he kept an eye out for them as, planting after planting, the rice surged from the mud.

About the Author

Terence Clarke is the author of *My Father in the Night* and *The Day Nothing Happened*, both published by Mercury House. His stories have appeared in numerous literary journals nationwide, including the *The Yale Review*, *The Denver Quarterly*, and *The Antioch Review*. He lived for several years in Borneo and now resides in San Francisco.

Text/Display Type:	Dante/Caslon Open Face
Text Designer:	Thomas Christensen
Compositor:	Philip Bronson
Editors:	Thomas Christensen, Cynthia Gitter, and Janet Mowery
Printer/Binder:	Haddon Craftsmen